A Most Compromising Position

Colly knew that the world might think it shocking that Lord Ethan Raymond lay in a bed in Colly's house. But surely even the most strait-laced members of society would understand that the dashing lord had been injured in a fall and could not be moved.

But now the situation was a bit more difficult to explain. Colly had been attempting to give Lord Raymond nourishment when he had fainted. And now his dead weight lay upon her hair, tying her to him despite her hardest efforts.

What would happen if a maid found her in this most compromising position? Even worse, what would happen when Lord Raymond came to his senses, only to have them roused by her beside him in his bed?

Only one thing was sure, Colly thought as, weary from her efforts to free herself, she settled her body next to Lord Raymond's lean and powerful frame: *It was going to be a long, long night. . . .*

SIGNET REGENCY ROMANCE
Coming in September 1995

Emma Lange
Exeter's Daughter

Barbara Hazard
Dangerous Deceits

Gayle Buck
Lady Althea's Bargain

The Marrying Season

by

Martha Kirkland

A SIGNET BOOK

SIGNET
Published by the Penguin Group
Penguin Books USA Inc., 375 Hudson Street,
New York, New York 10014, U.S.A.
Penguin Books Ltd, 27 Wrights Lane,
London W8 5TZ, England
Penguin Books Australia Ltd, Ringwood,
Victoria, Australia
Penguin Books Canada Ltd, 10 Alcorn Avenue,
Toronto, Ontario, Canada M4V 3B2
Penguin Books (N.Z.) Ltd, 182–190 Wairau Road,
Auckland 10, New Zealand

Penguin Books Ltd, Registered Offices:
Harmondsworth, Middlesex, England

First published by Signet, an imprint of Dutton Signet,
a division of Penguin Books USA Inc.

First Printing, August, 1995
10 9 8 7 6 5 4 3 2 1

To my all-the-time hero,
Tal Kirkland
and to our wonderful daughters,
Lorraine and Dawn Ellen.

Chapter 1

"Lud, Ethan," Mr. Durwin Harrison said, slapping his plump, satin-clad knee, "I am glad you have abandoned your estates and that school business, if only for a short while. You are too serious by half since your father's demise, and this is a great time to come up to town, even though it is summer. The place is abuzz with the frantic machinations of the royal dukes, all of them suddenly in a race to see who can marry first and produce the heir to the throne."

Mr. Harrison's ruddy face creased with laughter. "The Duke of Clarence is especially amusing and has made himself the butt of half the jokes at the clubs. After having proposed marriage to the exquisite Miss Tylneylong, then Miss Mercer Elphinstone, and then that heiress, Miss Wykeham—and been spurned by all three—now he has agreed to this arranged betrothal to some obscure German princess."

Ethan Delacourt Bradford, the sixth Baron Raymond, leaned against a handsome Adam mantel, his muscular arms folded across his chest, and stared unseeingly at some object across the candlelit book room. For all the attention he paid the chatter of his dinner companion and lifelong friend, he might as well have been alone.

"I tell you, Ethan, the betting book at White's is filled with wagers on how soon after clapping eyes upon her betrothed, the princess Adelaide turns and flees the country." His loud guffaw resounded in the late-night quiet of the room. "I laid a pony she would balk on the evening of the third day. Wanted to lay my blunt on the first evening, but old Coruthers was there ahead of me, already had a monkey on it."

Noticing that his friend had not shared in his laughter, Mr. Harrison gave his attention to the crystal decanter that had been placed on the Pembroke table at his elbow by Ethan's estimable butler, Yardley. He filled his glass, sniffed the excellent bouquet of the brandy, then tasted the smooth liquid, letting it glide slowly down his throat.

As he resettled himself in the leather-covered wing chair, one plump leg draped negligently over the chair arm, he eyed a plate of freshly baked cakes. His friend's wine cellar, second to none in London, was only one of the delights of Raymond House. Ethan's chef was coveted by half the hostesses in London.

"Not that I blame Prinny for giving his support to this scheme to marry off his brothers," he continued, a macaroon halfway to his mouth. "The country must have an heir. But watching the royal dukes—all of them middle-aged, and at least one of them distressingly corpulent—scouring Europe for eligible, nubile princesses is more than a sensible man can endure with a straight face."

When Lord Raymond vouchsafed no reply, Mr. Harrison set the macaroon aside and licked an errant crumb from his full bottom lip. "If I am keeping you from your bed, dear boy, just say so. I can take myself back to my lodgings in a trice. Wouldn't want to overstay my welcome."

"Your pardon," Ethan replied, pushing away from the mantel and stretching to his full six feet. "I am afraid my mind was wandering." A smile played at the corners of his well-shaped lips, softening the angular face that one disappointed young lady had stigmatized as too forbidding by half. "Blame it on my advanced age."

"Certainly," Mr. Harrison replied affably, wistfully eyeing the cut of Lord Raymond's blue evening coat and the way it fit so smoothly across his friend's broad, athletic shoulders. "I will blame it on anything you like. Although for a man of your advanced years—thirty, is it not?—you seem remarkably fit."

Ethan's smile vanished. "The guardianship of a harebrained younger brother obliges me to keep fit."

"I might have known your preoccupation would have something to do with that young paperskull. Ever since the Bag Wig sent him down from school, Reggie's been up to every rig. Been amusing himself boxing the watch, has he?"

"I wish it were that simple."

"Well, I remember you threatened to draw and quarter the lad if he ever again visited one of those havy-cavy gaming hells, so that cannot be what has got you blue deviled." Sitting up, Mr. Harrison brushed stray morsels of cake from his silver brocade waistcoat, then took a sip of his brandy. "So if it ain't pranks, and it ain't gambling, that leaves only the fair sex." He chuckled. "Never tell me the lad has taken a page out of the royal book and gotten himself betrothed?"

"You are too sharp for me, Winny."

"Egad, Ethan! I was merely funning. Reggie cannot be above eighteen." He shook his head, then was forced to rearrange a carrot-colored lock of his carefully pomaded Brutus. "The lad's attic must be to let."

"No. Reggie is just heedless. He rushes his fences, then considers the consequences later. Much later."

"But some consequences will not wait for later, betrothals being among that number. They have a nasty way of catching up with a fellow."

Ethan's thick, dark eyebrows lifted in displeasure. "As you say, it has caught up with him."

"Naturally. And might one hazard a guess that in the light of day, the parson's mousetrap lost the allure it held by candlelight?"

"I can always depend upon your grasp of the central point, my friend."

Mr. Harrison rolled his slightly protuberant eyes heavenward. "And now, I presume, your brother wishes you to extricate him from his latest folly."

"That is his wish . . . hopefully before word of it reaches our mother."

Ethan walked over to the massive desk that dominated the far end of the room. Once there he withdrew a piece of paper from the top drawer, then returned to his place beside the empty fireplace. "Of course, there can be no question of legalities in this matter. Reggie has not obtained his majority and could not enter into a formal betrothal contract without my consent." He stared at the paper with its broken wafer. "Unfortunately, there is a further complication."

"If you are worried about tittle-tattle, dear boy, I should not think the story would be more than a nine-days' wonder. Not with the royal dukes supplying the ton with *on dits* around the clock. Compared to royal betrothals, the near betrothal of a mere lad should prove rather insipid fare for the gossipmongers."

"I hope you are right, Winny. However, the complication to which I refer is of another nature." Ethan ran his hand through his midnight black hair. "It seems my brother sealed the bargain with the family betrothal ring."

Mr. Harrison choked on his brandy. "The Bradford Diamond! Egad, Ethan, you cannot be serious. The demmed ring is worth a king's ransom." In deference to his friend's feelings, he made no mention of the fact that the ring's rightful owner was the Bradford heir—Ethan.

"Reggie knows he had no right to the ring," he said, as though reading his friend's thoughts, "and he has begged my pardon."

Mr. Harrison kept his tongue between his teeth on

the subject of heedless cubs who acted badly, then expected pardon for the mere asking.

"The important thing now, Winny, is getting the ring back."

"I should rather think it would be. But what of the young lady? Has she a *tendre* for the lad, do you think?"

Ethan shook his head. "That I cannot answer."

"Do we know the chit?"

"*I* do not, and that worries me. I have asked a few discreet questions here in town, but no one appears to be acquainted with the family."

Pondering this new information, Mr. Harrison asked, "Might the lad have got himself entangled with some demi rep? Some seasoned adventuress who would entrap him thinking to extract money from the Bradford coffers?"

Ethan's face was grim. "That could be her design. Anything is possible. I do not even know the person's given name."

"But surely Reggie told you—"

"All I know is that she is a Miss Sommes, from a village near Canterbury." He unfolded the piece of paper he held in his hand. "Her first name is illegible."

Mr. Harrison stared at the paper that had been abused by repeated folding and unfolding. "Am I to assume that your brother took the course of least resistance and opened his budget in a letter?"

Ethan nodded. "It was delivered this morning to Raymond Park. I left for town within the hour, but by the time I got here, Reggie and that addlepated school chum of his had already taken themselves off on a repairing lease, their destination unknown."

He passed the mangled letter to Mr. Harrison. "See what you make of the chit's name. It is there in the last paragraph."

Mr. Harrison held the paper close to the branch of candles nearest his chair and attempted to decipher the youthful scratches on the page. "Demmed scrawl," he muttered, "and half the words have been crossed out or written over."

He moved the candelabra closer and reread the paragraph. "The letters are difficult to make out, but it looks like the name might be Gilly, or Milly. No, wait. It is Molly. No . . . " He returned the letter to Ethan. "Sorry, dear boy, it could be anything."

Ethan held the letter over one of the candles until yellow-blue flames licked the edge of the paper. When it was well caught, he tossed the paper into the empty fireplace. The flames devoured the missive in a matter of seconds. "Whatever her name, I must find her."

"Of course. But how do you plan to do that?"

"Since my only lead is Canterbury, I will have to go there. My mother has an elderly cousin who resides in the town; I will stop by the old girl's place and see if she is acquainted with the Sommes family. Once I locate the family, and pay them off if necessary, I will tell Miss Gilly-Milly-Molly to hand over the Bradford Diamond."

"And what if there is no Sommes family? What if the person is, in fact, an adventuress who has taken the ring and bolted to the Continent? One might live a luxurious life on the proceeds from such a stone."

A flash of anger darkened Ethan's brown eyes, making them appear cold and dangerous. "If she has run, I will find her. And if she has sold the ring, I will make her rue the day she decided to cheat Ethan Bradford."

Chapter 2

"That devil! That vicious black devil!" Miss Columbine Sommes slammed the French doors leading from the garden into the summer morning room and leaned her slim yet shapely back against the cool panes of glass. Her breath came in ragged gasps, and her gray-green eyes blazed with anger.

In her hand she clutched a once fetching gray hat whose teal green feather hung limp and broken. The skirt of her gray Directoire riding habit was in similarly sad condition, and when she let the hem fall to the carpet, it showed a deep rent. Her light brown hair, which had tumbled from its customary loose knot at the nape of her neck, fell about her back and shoulders in disarray.

"That horse should be shot!" she announced to the astonished older lady who sat on the yellow silk sofa near the window. "He broke free of his box again and charged at Essex Maid just as the groom threw me into the Maid's saddle. If the lad had not kept his wits about him and dragged me from harm's way, I might have been killed."

Miss Petunia Montrose, a spinster of some sixty

plus summers, rushed to her niece's side. "Colly, my dear, are you hurt?"

The sight of her great aunt's distress blunted the edges of Colly's anger. "Nothing to signify, Aunt Pet, but only because Papa's new Arab was thwarted in his attempt."

The older lady relaxed. "That beast—the stallion, of course, not your dear papa—should be removed as soon as possible. And so I shall inform Sir Wilfred the moment he returns from his regimental reunion. It is a miracle you did not sustain serious injury."

Colly patted her aunt's hand, then tossed the mangled hat onto a leather reading chair whose sole purpose in the room seemed to be as a collector of abandoned articles. "And just look at my habit, Aunt Pet. It is ruined."

"I hope it may be," declared Miss Montrose, pleased with this fortuitous introduction of a topic she had hoped to discuss with her niece as soon as she could arrange it.

She frowned at Colly's somber habit, then fingered the skirt of her own new dress, a confection whose green stripes—*pistache*, the dressmaker called the new color—perfectly matched the jean half boots that peeped from beneath the flounced hem. "With mourning for our beloved Princess Charlotte now at an end, you have no need to wear that dreary gray."

Miss Montrose smoothed the *pistache* again. "It is

most uplifting to the spirit to be arrayed in colors once again."

Colly smiled. "Arrayed like the flowers we are, Aunt Petunia?"

The lady nodded her head, acknowledging the sally regarding the peculiarity of the Montrose family in naming all its females after flowers. "Tease me if you will, my dear, but colors are in. And this one, as your father would say, is all the crack."

Colly schooled her lips not to betray her amusement at her aunt's use of cant.

"I know you are trying not to smile, my dear, but let me assure you, the state of your wardrobe is no laughing matter. It is in sad need of refurbishing. I wish you had not declined your mother's invitation to accompany her and your sister to London to be outfitted for the coming season."

Colly shook her head. "It is my sister's season, Aunt, not mine. My presence will not be required for above one or two parties, and for those I can just as well have my clothes made closer to home."

"In Canterbury?" Miss Montrose asked hopefully. "My dressmaker has some marvelous new patterns."

The lady hurried over to the sofa and retrieved the newspaper she had been perusing when her niece burst into the room. "Read this," she said, pushing the paper into Colly's hands as further inducement to the trip. "The article says Princess Adelaide of Saxe-Meiningen and her mother, the duchess, are expected in Canterbury in a few days' time. Their boat will dock at Deal, and from there they will travel by coach to Canterbury, where they have planned to rest for one night before continuing the journey to London."

The maiden lady sighed. "If we were in Canterbury, we might see the princess. Or," she added hopefully, "we might even be fortunate enough to glimpse the Duke of Clarence as he escorts his future bride to London. Only think of it, Colly, a beautiful princess and her handsome prince charming."

Colly returned the newspaper to her aunt. "I am loath to disabuse you of your romantic dreams, Aunt Pet, but whatever may prove true of the young German princess, I can assure you, the Duke of Clarence is no prince charming. I saw him on more than one occasion the year I had my come-out, and I am persuaded that he has not grown any more princely in the seven years since I beheld him last.

"But," she added when she saw the disappointment on her aunt's face, "you are correct regarding my need for a new wardrobe. And if you wish to join the vulgar throngs as they stare at the duke and his unsuspecting princess, I have no objections to the plan. By all means, let us hasten to Canterbury without further delay. We'll make a holiday of it. After we visit all the shops, we can mingle with the masses and ogle royalty to our hearts' content."

When she was able to disengage herself from her aunt's enthusiastic embrace, Colly walked over to the door that opened onto the main hallway. "While I change into one of my shamefully dull dresses, Aunt Pet, you might have Wexler send one of the grooms to Canterbury to book us rooms at the inn before they are all taken by the—"

The sentence ended abruptly as Colly halted just in time to avoid collision with the elderly butler who stood poised, ready to knock at the door she had just opened. "Begging your pardon, Miss Colly."

"And I yours, Wexler." When he did not stand aside to allow her to pass, she asked, "Was there something you wished?"

"There is a visitor, Miss Colly. I have shown him to the small drawing room." The butler held a silver salver upon which lay a calling card of pristine whiteness. "It is Lord Raymond," he informed her before she could reach for the card.

Assuming the visitor was one of Sir Wilfred's cronies, she left the card untouched. "Did you inform his lordship that Papa is from home?"

The butler closed his eyes in the resigned attitude of retainers who are asked foolish questions by persons they have known from the cradle. "His lordship did not ask for Sir Wilfred, Miss Colly, he specifically asked to be announced to *Miss* Sommes."

"But I am not acquainted with a Lord Raymond."

"Shall I tell his lordship you are from home?"

"No, don't do that, Wexler." Sighing, Colly pushed a thick fall of hair away from her face. "I will see him, but I cannot do so looking like this. Please offer the gentleman some refreshment, and advise him I will join him directly."

As the butler turned to do her bidding, Colly was startled to discover the visitor standing in the hallway watching her. He must have been doing so for

several moments. And far from showing repentance
for his breach of etiquette in not staying in the room
to which he had been shown, the man raised a sardonic brow, then made Colly a bow that was almost
insolent in its brevity.

"Do not change on my account," he said. "This is
not a social call."

At first Colly returned the visitor's stare, but as his
angry brown eyes raked her from head to toe, lingering impertinently on her bosom and rounded hips
before looking his fill of her tumbled curls, she finally yielded and lowered her gaze. But even as she
looked away, her face grew warm with dawning
recognition.

It was him. Him. Her brain could not credit the
evidence of her eyes. *He stood before her.* Her lungs
seemed to forget their primary function, and when
she finally found her voice, she was not surprised to
hear the breathlessness in it. "You wished to see me,
Mr. Br—er, Lord Raymond?"

"If you are Miss Sommes."

Colly forced herself to respond with a degree of
normalcy she was far from feeling. "I am, sir."

Ethan knew she was the person he had come to
see—the person to whom his brother had given the
Bradford Diamond—he had heard the butler call her
Miss Colly. That must have been what Reggie
scrawled in his letter. Not Molly but Colly.

Ethan stared at her, he couldn't help himself.
Demme, but she was a diamond herself! A far cry
from the insipid chit he had hoped to find. This was
a woman. A vibrant, beautiful woman. Her sculpted

brow and slender nose lent her a look of serenity, while her soft, full lips and mysterious eyes hinted at the passion that lay just beneath her calm exterior. Studying the mass of curls that tumbled about her shoulders, he could imagine the pleasure a man would derive from burying his face in that magnificent hair.

Poor Reggie. The boy had not stood a chance. A woman who looked like that could get almost anything she wanted from a man; a green boy would be putty in her hands.

"How do you do, Lord Raymond?" said an older lady, bringing Ethan's thoughts back to the business at hand. "Pray come in. I am Miss Montrose, Lady Sommes' aunt. And Colly's aunt, too, of course, since she is Violet's—that is to say Lady Sommes'— daughter."

He bowed over the lady's hand, showing her the grace of manners he had forgotten in her niece's presence. "Your servant, Miss Montrose."

"Wexler," Miss Montrose said, "please ask cook to prepare a tea tray." She looked at Ethan. "Or perhaps something stronger, Lord Raymond?"

"No, thank you, ma'am. Actually, there is a matter I must discuss with Miss Sommes. A matter of business."

Colly roused herself from the shocked stupor she had fallen into once she had recognized the caller as Ethan Bradford. "A matter of business, with me? I am afraid you have the advantage of me, sir, as I have no idea to what business you refer."

Ethan marveled at that just-right note of bewilderment in her voice. He could almost believe she spoke the truth. Almost.

Though he had hoped to speak privately with her, she crossed the room and chose a seat next to her aunt on the sofa, gracefully resting her hands in her lap and giving him her full attention. He marveled at her composure. The skirt of her riding habit was torn, her hair fell all about her shoulders, and she had to know that he had come to retrieve the Bradford Diamond, yet she appeared calm, unruffled. Anyone observing her would have thought she had not a care in the world, that she had nothing to worry about from him. Lud, but she was a cool jade.

He decided to cut to the chase. "I have come for the ring."

The two women exchanged glances.

"The ring?" Miss Sommes repeated.

So, she wants to play the charade out. She would catch cold on that. It should not take him long to convince her that he was more than a match for her. He was no green schoolboy to be taken in by a beautiful face and a shapely figure.

At Miss Montrose's invitation, Ethan lowered himself into a tapestry-covered chair beside a tripod table on which rested a Sevres vase depicting a medieval battle scene. Hoping the deftly painted battle was not some omen of things to come, he trailed a nonchalant finger along the bronze base of the vase.

"Miss Sommes," he began, trying a new tack, "you are acquainted with my brother."

She shook her head. "I do not believe I have had the pleasure, sir."

Try as he might to resist, Ethan felt the corners of his mouth pull into a smile. The beauty would make a formidable whist player; she looked so demmed believable. "Come, now, ma'am. We will get nowhere if you continue in this—"

"Great heavens above!" Miss Montrose shouted, her attention caught by something she spied through the window just behind the sofa. "He has returned, Colly!"

With a gasp Miss Sommes pulled the lace curtains aside. "That devil! Now he is after—" She turned to face Ethan, her eyes wide with alarm. "Lord Raymond . . . sir . . . you came on horseback?"

Before he could answer her question, she rushed to the French doors and threw them open. "I am so sorry," she called over her shoulder, "but I fear my father's new stallion is attacking your horse!"

Ethan heard the threatening neigh of the stallion even before he reached the French doors and pushed Miss Sommes aside. By the time he heard the frightened squeal of his own horse, he was running at full speed toward the animal.

An enclosed garden led off the terrace beyond the French doors, but to the front of the house was a stretch of rolling green park. The stallion had chased Ethan's gelding from the stable, across the park, and now had it trapped between a thick hedge and a small ornamental pond. The gelding had no further place to run.

Two young stable lads reached the horses several moments before Ethan, and though they tried to shoo the stallion by shouting and waving pieces of blanket at his head, they waged a losing battle. They dared not get too close to the Arab, for to do so was to risk certain death from his lethal hooves.

Making an immediate appraisal of the situation and deducing that the lads were no match for the powerful steed, Ethan shouted for one of them to run back to the house and bring him a gun. He had no more than given the order when the stallion turned.

The enraged animal eyed Ethan suspiciously. Snorting and kicking, he covered the distance between him and his new quarry. Though Ethan waved his arms and shouted, the Arab, unafraid, raised his forelegs and brought them down with frightening force. Fortunately, Ethan was able to jump aside just as the hooves came down. Reacting instinctively, he threw himself at the animal's neck; then, with his fingers tangled in the stallion's mane, Ethan vaulted onto the horse's back.

The stallion bucked, trying to fling him off, but thanks to Ethan's fine physical condition, he was able to hold on. The Arab alternately bucked and reared, but all to no avail. Finally, in desperation the horse turned and bolted toward the open woods beyond the park.

With the danger to the young grooms and to his own animal now past, Ethan searched for a suitable place to jump clear of the four-legged devil. As fate would have it, just as he discovered such a place and released the Arab's mane, the stallion bucked one final time. The last thing Ethan remembered was the feeling of flying through the air.

Chapter 3

Thank heaven," Colly said, her soft voice sounding loud in the hushed late-night stillness, "you are conscious at last."

For the past two hours she had sat in a rosewood slipper chair in the corner of the shadowed bedroom, waiting for Lord Raymond to regain consciousness. Very soon the dawn would begin to paint the sky with her soft pinks and grays, but for the moment all was dark, save for the lone candle that flickered on the tripod table to Colly's right. Her eyelids had grown heavy, and she must have closed them for a second, for the book of poems she had been reading earlier fell to the carpeted floor with a soft thud. As she bent to retrieve the book, something made her glance toward the ornately carved tester bed on which the injured man lay.

His eyes were open. He was watching her.

Setting the book on the table, Colly hurried across the room to stand beside the bed with its shot silk hangings. She took a steadying breath to dispel the frightening recollection of how Lord Raymond had looked when they found him lying in the woods, his face deathly pale and his coat covered with blood. At first, when he did not move, she had been afraid he might be . . .

The possibilities were too horrible to contemplate, so with a calm she did not feel, she laid her hand on his brow as if he suffered from nothing worse than a head cold. His skin was hot, but not, thank heaven, as hot as it had been earlier.

"You have a fever, sir, which cannot, of course, be comfortable, and for which I humbly beg your pardon. But I am happy to report that aside from the fever, and a few minor cuts, that vile-tempered stallion managed to inflict upon you nothing more serious than a badly pulled shoulder. And the doctor assured us before he left that you will survive all your maladies."

When she started to remove her hand, Lord Raymond reached up and captured it, then placed it against his warm cheek. "Mmm," he murmured groggily, holding her hand within his and nuzzling his face into it, "that feels good."

Colly's neck grew almost as warm as Lord Raymond's forehead. Perhaps her taking a turn in the sick room had been a mistake. Aunt Pet and the housekeeper had divided between them the task of watching over their injured visitor, but Colly had insisted upon taking at least one turn, so that her elderly aunt could stretch out upon her bed for several hours. At the moment Colly was not sure that had been an altogether wise plan, for when the patient began to nuzzle her hand, she remembered that he was also a man—a man with a reputation for success with the ladies.

It was a moot point almost immediately, since Lord Raymond closed his eyes and slept again. He still held her hand to his face, and Colly was loath to pull it away. She told herself it was fear of disturbing him that kept her hand in his, but honesty compelled her to admit that it was the pleasure of feeling his masculine cheek against her palm that kept her still.

She studied his face. Seven years ago she had thought him the handsomest man she had ever seen, and by anyone's standards he was still handsome. But his face had changed since she saw him last. Time had sketched small, almost invisible lines in the outside corners of his eyes, and the angle of his square jaw seemed sharper now. Life, or perhaps responsibilities, had chiseled his features, making them appear more determined, more commanding, and making the man seem less approachable.

The first time she saw Ethan he had been a young man of twenty-three, dressed in his brilliant Hussar uniform. The occasion was the ball for another young lady also making her come-out that season, and all the ladies in the ballroom were casting sheep's eyes at him. His father had only recently inherited the title, as well as a considerable fortune, from a cousin, and suddenly Ethan was the most sought-after bachelor of the season, the *premier parti*. His very presence at a ball branded it a success.

When Ethan asked Colly to partner him in a

waltz, she had been rendered speechless. No one, herself included, knew why he chose her when there were so many livelier girls present; perhaps it was because she had not tried to attract his attention. Whatever his reasons, she still remembered that dance.

Even now she could recall how she had felt when he put his gloved hand at her back—embarrassed and at the same time thrilled. She had never waltzed with a man before. In her memory she heard again the beauty of the orchestra music as it filled the crowded ballroom, and she felt again the heady, delicious warmth that permeated her entire body as Ethan whirled her around the room in his strong embrace.

Unfortunately, her joy soon turned to embarrassment. Gauche and tongue-tied with awe, the seventeen-year-old Colly had been unable to think of a word to say to her dashing partner, and though he had tried valiantly to engage her in conversation and thanked her politely after their dance was finished, she knew he had been bored. It had bruised her girlish heart to admit it, but she was certain that by the time he returned her to her mama, he had already forgotten her name. But she never forgot *his* name. At that time he had been Ethan Bradford.

Yesterday, when Wexler announced him as Lord Raymond, it was several moments before Colly recognized him as Ethan Bradford. She was not surprised that he had shown no such recognition of her.

Now, as she studied his face, he moved, releasing her hand. Almost immediately he began to moan and turn his head back and forth as if seeking a cool spot on the pillow. As she had done earlier, Colly soaked a cloth in the bowl of rose water Wexler had left on the wrought iron washstand, then gently laid the cloth on Ethan's forehead. The coolness seemed to soothe him, so she continued applying damp cloths until he grew calm once again.

She thought he was sleeping, but he surprised her by asking for something to drink.

"Of course," she replied. "You may have the barley water the doctor ordered for you, or if you prefer it, my aunt prepared some lemonade."

He gave her a sleepy smile so sweet it nearly took her breath away. "The lemonade, please."

Colly turned away so he could not see her confusion. Then, calling herself an idiot, she went over to a dresser where a crystal pitcher of lemonade was set beside a brown jug of barley water. She poured the lemonade into a glass and carried it back to the patient.

"Here you are, Lord Raymond. Perhaps a refreshing drink will help you rest more easily."

Of course, it became apparent immediately that getting the drink inside the man might prove a problem. His right shoulder was wrapped snugly, and his arm was bound to his chest by further bandaging to keep him from injuring the shoulder if he became restless and thrashed about. Wrapped this way, he was, for all practical purposes, a large mummy.

"Let me try, Lord Raymond, if I can get my arm beneath your shoulders without causing you too much pain. If all goes well, perhaps you can then raise your head enough to have your drink."

The plan was more easily devised than executed. Ethan being a large man, Colly struggled mightily just to lift him sufficiently. Slaking his thirst was another matter altogether. As fate would have it, the glass had no more than touched the patient's fevered lips when his eyes closed and he lost consciousness again.

As Ethan fell back against his pillow, Colly found herself unable to withstand the pull of his powerful shoulders; she and the lemonade both pitched forward. The glass and its contents landed on the carpet on the far side of the bed, while the ministering angel landed across Ethan's chest.

Slightly breathless from the unexpected tumble, and very much embarrassed, Colly warned herself not to make a piece of work over nothing. All she needed to do to extricate herself was to slip her arm from beneath the unconscious man's shoulders. A simple plan. Regrettably, it did not serve, for she soon discovered that to remove her arm she must first lift her head from his chest. And lifting her head was impossible. The chignon she wore dressed loosely at the nape of her neck was caught fast by the pins that held Ethan's bandages in place.

Momentarily thwarted, but still not thinking herself at *point non plus*, Colly reached behind her head with her right hand. She pulled. She tugged. She yanked the imprisoned tresses. All to no avail. She could not free her hair. If anything, she was more surely caught than before. Frustrated, she jerked her

head with all her strength, hoping to disentangle
herself, but the pain that rewarded that idiotic effort
convinced her there must be a better way.

Fifteen minutes later, when Colly still had not discovered that better way, the truth of her situation
struck her forcefully. She was caught like an animal
in a snare, with no hope for release. Ethan's room
was in the guest wing, so yelling for her aunt would
serve no purpose, and to make bad matters worse,
her lower back was crying out for relief from her
awkward posture half on and half off the bed.

Colly yielded to the cries of her cramped muscles
and dragged her aching legs up onto Ethan's bed,
stretching her body along the length of his. She felt
the tears of relief dampen her face, but she dashed
the tears away with the back of her free hand, angry
with herself for getting into this stupid and extremely compromising predicament.

"All it needs now," she muttered, "is for one of the
maids to walk in and find me thus, lying beside
Ethan with my arm around his neck and my head
seemingly nestled on his chest."

To be rescued or not to be rescued? That quite distressing rub irritated her brain, until it was literally
yanked from her thoughts when Ethan became restless and almost wrenched her head off.

To her further dismay, she noticed that muted
morning light had begun to peep around the edges
of the velvet curtains drawn across the leaded windows. The maids would be stirring within the next
few minutes, and should one of them come to this
room, Colly would be discovered in what would ap-

pear to be flagrante delicto. And when discovered, she would be hopelessly compromised.

She resigned herself to her fate. There was no way out of this coil.

But, she vowed to herself, *no matter what happens, I will not be party to a forced marriage.* No sooner was the vow taken than Colly heard the door open. The next sound she heard was a gasp.

"Colly!"

"Aunt Pet," she whispered, almost weak with relief, "thank heaven it is you."

"What does this mean? My dear, have you lost all sense of—"

"Shh. If there is a maid with you, please do not let her enter. I vow I will explain everything to your satisfaction later, but for now, speed is of the essence. I need assistance."

Her aunt approached the bed cautiously. "What do—"

"Go around to the other side of the bed and see if you can get me loose. I am caught by the hair."

The maiden lady did as she was bidden. "I see the problem," she said immediately, "but I cannot free you without scissors. Be patient a little longer, my dear, I will return in a trice."

Within minutes Colly heard her aunt's return. She must have run, for her breathing was audible in the silence of the room. When Colly begged her not to waste precious moments on finesse, her aunt ruthlessly sawed through the offending strands of hair.

"Done," she whispered when all the strands were severed.

Freed at last, Colly lost no time in slipping her captured arm from beneath Ethan's shoulders and getting as far across the room as possible. While she cradled her left arm in her right hand, gritting her teeth as slivers of returning sensation pierced her flesh, her aunt went to the door and peeked out into the hallway.

"It is still deserted," the lady said. "If you hurry, perhaps you may reach your bedchamber before your maid arrives with your morning chocolate."

Giving her rescuer a quick hug, Colly said, "Thank you, Aunt. My mind was at sixes and sevens, and I could not think how it might be—"

"Hush, child. We have no time for talk. You must hurry. If you can contrive to be back under your covers before your maid arrives, no one need know you ever left your bed."

Obediently, Colly sped down the corridor and around the corner to her own room. Mindful of her aunt's sensible advice, she slipped out of her dress and shift then donned her nightgown and wrapper. She was sitting up in bed when her maid arrived ten minutes later.

Lord Raymond woke slowly. He opened his eyes, then closed them again when daggers of morning sunlight coming through the windows stabbed his pupils and assaulted his skull. His fever was gone, but his head felt as though someone had used it for a cricket ball. And he hurt in so many other places that the absence of the fever hardly seemed a blessing. He lay quietly. He could do nothing more with his torso encased in bandages.

Concentrating, he tried to focus, though his brain was less than cooperative. He recalled being tossed by the stallion, but he remembered little else . . . except for that one time when he woke with some degree of lucidity to find Miss Sommes sitting in a chair reading.

Ethan thought he remembered her asking him if he wanted something to drink, but perhaps that was a hallucination. The hallucinations had been many and varied, several of them involving troll-like creatures who jeered at him mercilessly from behind doors and bedposts. Once when he thought himself awake, Ethan had even imagined that Miss Sommes was snuggled beside him in the bed, her arms wrapped around him and her head resting on his chest.

Later that morning Colly returned to Ethan's room, followed by a maid who carried a small tray of steaming chocolate and toast. It needed more courage than she had known she possessed to enter his room again, knowing that he was awake and his fever a thing of the past, for she had no idea how he would receive her. What if, somehow, he knew she had been in his bed the night before? And if he knew, what if he thought she had used his illness to compromise him into a marriage proposal?

She would certainly understand such an assumption on his part. Looking at their circumstances through the eyes of the *haut ton*, Lord Raymond was a matrimonial prize, one who might look as high as he dared for an eligible *parti*. He was handsome, wealthy, and from an old and illustrious family, while Miss Columbine Sommes was a country nobody. Moreover, a nobody on the brink of being an ape leader.

Not that she had not had offers for her hand; she had, one as recently as this past Michaelmas. But she could hardly expect the world to believe she was unmarried by choice. Nor could she expect anyone to believe that she preferred life as a spinster to life in a loveless or, even worse, a one-sided marriage.

Colly wanted no part of a marriage in which the affections were unequal. One needed only to observe her parents to witness the result of such a marriage. Sir Wilfred, a good though blustery man, worshiped his beautiful, and much younger, wife, but she did not return his feelings. Not that Colly's mother did not like and respect her husband; she most certainly did, but therein lay the pain: Adoration reciprocated by mere fondness was a constant ache for the one who truly loved.

Colly would rather ape-lead for an eternity.

When she entered Ethan's room, she found him propped up against a stack of pillows. He had been placed in the butler's questionable hands to be shaved and brushed, and he now wore one of Sir Wilfred's most unfortunate dressing gowns—a rather florid creation of red game birds in flight against a backdrop of golden sunset. His lordship had obviously survived Wexler's ministrations, and though still pale, he was once again in command of his faculties, a man to be reckoned with.

Colly felt the strength of his personality from several feet away, and her pulse raced at the sight of him, virile and relaxed, watching her from his bed. Remembering how she had lain next to him in that bed, she almost turned craven and ran. The maid must have felt similarly shy, for she placed the small tray on the bedside table, bobbed a curtsy, then fled from the room.

"Is that chocolate I smell?" Ethan asked, effectively staying Colly's footsteps. "If so, pray delay no longer. Pour me a cup, Miss Sommes, for I am as parched as the Sahara and feel as if it has been at least a fortnight since I last had a meal."

He asked for food.

Colly's entire body trembled with relief. He obviously did not know she had been in his bed, for if he knew, he would be demanding his horse, or his solicitor, not toast and chocolate.

After calming herself by filling her lungs, then slowly releasing the breath, Colly moved over to the tray abandoned by the maid. She touched the Chelsea Rose pot to test its temperature, grateful for any task that kept her from looking into his eyes. As she poured the chocolate into the translucent cup, then turned to offer it to Lord Raymond, she hoped her smile was warm enough to convince him she had no reason to feel discomforted in his presence.

"The return of one's appetite," she said, "is the second sign that one is on the mend."

"The second?" he said, raising the cup to his lips

and drinking deeply. His intent gaze never left Colly's face, and it was all she could do to maintain her tranquil facade. "And what, madam, is the first sign?"

Colly felt her cheeks grow warm. "The first sign," she answered, wishing she had not introduced the subject, "is peaceful sleep."

"And did I sleep peacefully?"

She nodded, then looked away; she wanted no more talk of sleep and beds.

Ethan watched her. Miss Sommes looked discomfited, almost as though she found the subject of a gentleman's sleep habits an embarrassing topic. If he had not known her for an adventuress, an enchantress of green youths, Ethan might have been lulled into believing her the innocent she looked.

Avoiding his gaze, the object of his study turned away from the bedside table and crossed the room to sit in the slipper chair she had occupied the night before when he awoke and found her reading. As she turned, her movements caused a hint of lemon verbena to waft Ethan's way, and the subtle fragrance recalled that hallucinatory dream, the dream in which Miss Sommes had slept in his arms. In his dream she had felt soft and warm, and quite deliciously—

Ethan forced his thoughts away from last night's fantasies, refusing to let himself be distracted by the woman's charms. After all, charm was the stock and trade of an adventuress. And being a wealthy bachelor, Ethan had seen all the tricks.

Of course, he had never seen eyes that particular

color before—not quite gray, not quite green. And he liked the way she wore her hair. It was a classical style, pulled back at the nape of her neck, but with little tendrils resting against her cheeks. Also, there was a quiet dignity about her. For an adventuress, Miss Sommes had an undeniable elegance.

Ethan was in the process of reminding himself that the woman knew nothing of elegance—that she had tricked his gullible brother into an engagement and now held the Bradford Diamond in her possession—when the maid returned, bobbed a respectful curtsy, then informed her mistress that Dr. Beckman had come to check on the patient.

With a look in her gray-green eyes that clearly bespoke relief that an ordeal was over, Miss Sommes stood rather hastily and hurried to the door. "I will leave you to Dr. Beckman's kind offices, Lord Raymond."

Ethan forced a smile to his lips. If the woman thought her ordeal was over, he would disabuse her of that notion quickly enough; her ordeal with him had only just begun. He might be grateful for her care of him last night, but not grateful enough to allow her to keep the Bradford Diamond. "You will come back later, will you not, Miss Sommes? You and I both know there is a matter of some importance we must discuss."

Miss Sommes' eyes grew wide, wary, reminding Ethan momentarily of a cornered fawn. "Believe me, sir, there is not the least need for—" She stopped

whatever she had been about to say and greeted the
man whose footsteps he heard just outside the door.

The doctor exchanged a minimum of pleasantries
with the woman, then closed the door and approached the bed. The man's black coat was wrinkled and his shirt points and once starched neck
cloth sagged limply about his throat. His eyes were
red-rimmed from lack of sleep, and lines of fatigue
pulled his mouth into a frown.

"I have not seen my bed in two days, Lord Raymond, so you will forgive me if I am abrupt." With
that pronouncement the doctor laid his leather bag
down on the bedside table and pulled a wastebasket
within his reach.

"With your permission, my lord."

Waiting only for Ethan's nod, the doctor withdrew
the pillows from behind Ethan's back, then helped
him remove the startling dressing gown lent him
from Sir Wilfred's wardrobe.

"I dare say you will be pleased to be free of those
bandages, my lord."

While Ethan murmured something appropriate,
the doctor began removing the pins that held the
bandages in place. "Strange," he said, studying a
lock of hair twisted around one of the pins, "I wonder how that got there." He vouchsafed no further
comment, simply tossed both pin and lock onto the
bed table and unwound what seemed like miles of
bandage.

The man worked swiftly and competently. He
checked the injured shoulder, declared it to be as
right as a trivet, then fixed a sling around Ethan's

neck and recommended that he rest his arm in it for several days. "I suggest you protect that shoulder, my lord. And avoid any activities that might furnish further knocks on the head. Meanwhile," he added brusquely, "stay in bed for at least another day. That is an order!"

As soon as the door closed behind the good doctor, Ethan slid to the edge of the bed, being careful not to move too quickly and jar his throbbing shoulder. He eased his right arm from the sling and cautiously stretched it toward the bed table, where he found the pin with the lock of hair twisted around it. Not certain why it seemed important to him, he freed the snarled tress and laid it across the back of his hand where he could examine it.

The curl, about three inches long, was light brown, with streaks of gold shot through it. The ends, he noted, had been hacked rather crudely, as though done in haste. As he rubbed the silky strands between his fingers, a hint of lemon verbena teased his nostrils, and recollections of that hallucinatory dream rushed at him pell-mell—the dream in which Miss Sommes lay snuggled close to his chest.

His anger, when it came, was a mixture of fury at her and himself. "Damnation!" He fell back against the pillows, his body rigid with fury. "The oldest trick in the book!"

Several minutes passed before his anger subsided enough for him to put his thoughts in order. She was a clever puss, he would give her that, but she would need to show more resourcefulness than this to force Ethan Bradford into parson's mousetrap!

He laughed aloud. It was not a happy sound but derision aimed at himself. He had come to Sommes Grange thinking to rescue his naive brother from that Circe's grasp, only to run headlong into her clutches himself. What a fool he had been. After all the matchmaking mammas he had thwarted since succeeding to his father's title and wealth, he should have expected a trick of this kind. No adventuress worth her salt would settle for a younger son when the heir was stupid enough to play directly into her hands.

Ethan laid his head back against the pillows and tried to marshal his thoughts. There might yet be a way out of this muddle, but to find that way, he needed to consider the previous night from every angle. He remembered waking in the early hours of the morning and feeling a soft, warm body beside his. It was Miss Sommes, he was certain of that now. She had been stretched out full-length beside him with her arm beneath his shoulders.

"The curl must have caught on the pin when the minx put her head on my chest," he said aloud, a note of disgust in his voice. "Her with her shy smiles and her serene countenance. The woman could rival Mrs. Siddons!"

As he lay there mulling the scene over in his mind, one circumstance suddenly impressed Ethan as odd: He could not recall any other female ever having put her arm beneath his shoulders in that manner. She must have been devilish uncomfortable with her arm beneath his shoulders and her head on his chest. His smile was without humor. *Much of that kind of snuggling and she would be the one with the dislocated shoulder.*

Fast on the heels of that thought came another memory, one that made him pause and consider. "The lemonade!" he said finally, as though that explained it all. She had held him up, her arm behind his shoulders, so he could drink the lemonade. He remembered nothing after that.

"I must have passed out and fallen back against the pillows. And when I did, I must have pulled Miss Sommes down with me."

And that, he admitted to himself, was the truth of the matter. The lady had not caught her curl because she laid her head on his chest; it was the other way around. And she must have been obliged to wait in that position until someone came to free her.

He held the lock up and examined it again. "And the person who came to her rescue—the estimable Miss Montrose, I would guess—whacked the curl quickly to end her niece's imprisonment before I woke and found her in my bed."

After a moment he began to chuckle. As much as he hated to admit it, coping with the rather dubious distinction of being a matrimonial prize had turned him into a conceited oaf. Not only was Miss Sommes innocent of trying to compromise *him*, she had gone to some lengths to conceal the fact that *she* had been compromised.

Another thought occurred to him. If he had jumped to conclusions in this instance, might he also have jumped to others; might he have misjudged the lady regarding her betrothal to his brother? Since she obviously did not wish to marry himself, did she, indeed, cherish hopes of marrying his brother? What if she was not an adventuress after all, but simply an honest woman who had developed a genuine *tendre* for a younger man? Reggie could be a real charmer when he chose to be, and older ladies seemed especially susceptible to his boyish charm.

Not that Miss Sommes was old, of course, far from it, but she was several years older than Reggie. For some reason—a reason Ethan chose not to examine—the picture of Miss Sommes being in love with his scamp of a brother disturbed him more than his previous picture of her as an adventuress.

When this interesting introspection was interrupted by a knock at the door, Ethan shoved the curl beneath his pillow, then called to the visitor to enter. It was the curl's original owner. This time he had no doubts about the sincerity of Miss Sommes' embarrassment, even though she held her head as high as a queen's.

"You asked me to return, sir, to"—she hesitated only a moment—"to discuss a matter of some importance."

"Yes, ma'am, I did."

She walked over to the slipper chair and disposed herself primly, her hands folded in her lap. Her face was almost as pale as the blond lace that trimmed the sleeves and short waist of her lavender dress, but Ethan could not but admire the look of unruffled poise she managed to convey. She looked him directly in the eye.

"Lord Raymond, if I may speak first, I collect that you have remembered an incident which, for my sake, I wish you had forgot."

The lady had courage; he had to give her that. No simpering miss with a fit of the vapors, she went directly to the matter at hand.

"If you have any fears about having compromised me, sir, you may rest easy on that head. What happened last night was an unavoidable and completely blameless occurrence, and I see no reason why you, or I, should be bound for life by an episode that is much better forgotten by us both.

"Furthermore," she added, "my situation is not that of some schoolroom chit whose chances for the future have been blighted by being, uh, alone with a gentleman. I shall soon be five and twenty—quite 'on the shelf,' as the saying goes—and you may believe me when I tell you, sir, that I am not hanging out for a husband."

Ethan could only imagine how much that piece of plain speaking had cost her.

"And," she added, almost as an afterthought, "my affections are otherwise engaged."

Chapter 4

The devil take it! The lady was *in love* with his scapegrace of a brother.

What a coil. Here was Miss Sommes, considering herself pledged—her affections engaged—while Reggie gallivanted across the country, cavalierly thinking himself a free man. And here Ethan was, indebted to the lady for her kind ministrations to him, yet obliged to thank her by informing her of Reggie's defection.

Before this moment Ethan had not given any real thought to the possibility that Miss Sommes might have pledged her heart, that she might be hurt—perhaps devastated—to discover that Reggie did not return her affection. Ethan wished he had the thoughtless cub before him at this moment; he would cheerfully wring the lad's neck.

Unfortunately, the boy was not here, and it was left to Ethan to inform Miss Sommes that the betrothal was at an end. But not now, he decided. Not at this moment when she had come into his room so bravely to allay any fears he might have had about being compromised into matrimony. He could not, would not, repay such thoughtfulness by throwing embarrassing and painful news into her teeth.

Of course, he knew no way to soften the pain. Today or tomorrow her distress would be the same, but perhaps there was a way he could lessen her embarrassment. If she were more comfortable in his presence, if they were on terms of easy conversation, perhaps he could soften the blow of his brother's perfidy. With this objective in view, Ethan set his mind to winning Miss Sommes over.

He turned a smile of such warmth on her that Colly felt a flutter somewhere in the region of her heart. Of its own volition her smile answered his.

"So you see, sir," she reiterated, "you may put your concern for me to rest. I am already bespoken."

Colly was pleased with the result of her little white lie, especially since the story had come into her head full-blown, as it were. She wished she were privy to whatever thought had darkened Lord Raymond's eyes when she told him she loved someone, but it was enough that he had believed her and let down his guard. He had given her that heart-stopping smile, and now his warm brown eyes held a teasing glint that captured her attention.

"Lord Raymond," she said suspiciously, "I perceive that some question still remains in your mind. Did you wish to ask me something, sir?"

"Oh, no, ma'am," he replied nonchalantly. "Nothing at all, I assure you. That is to say, nothing of any *real* significance. Except . . ."

She mistrusted that careless tone in his voice, and as he had seen fit to avert his gaze, she could no longer look into his eyes and read his purpose. While she watched him, he stretched his left arm out before him and turned it this way and that, as if enjoying the play of sunlight upon the hideous birds depicted on his borrowed dressing gown.

She, too, studied the distressing juxtaposition of red and gold before returning her attention to Lord Raymond's now blasé face. "Except . . ." she repeated.

He feigned hurt pride. "I merely wondered, ma'am, how, after having been privileged to observe a bachelor so gloriously arrayed, you could possibly not wish to whisk him off to Gretna Green. Especially as you are a lady of such advanced years, and are, as you put it yourself, practically on the shelf. And I am, if you will excuse the pun, a peacock ripe for the plucking."

For a moment Colly was speechless. Then she noticed the slow smile that pulled at the corners of his mouth. She was hard pressed to control her own lips but somehow contrived not to answer his smile with one of her own.

"I will acknowledge, Lord Raymond, that the sight of a gentleman dressed in such a prime article of clothing must ordinarily make any maiden's heart flutter—be she ever so aged—but I assure you, in this instance my spinster's heart is whole and intact."

"Whew! I am the most fortunate of men. Who knows what unspeakable acts a less high-minded spinster might have committed upon the person of a bachelor thus arrayed."

"Who knows indeed, sir. By unspeakable acts . . . you meant homicide, did you not?"

"Uh, no, ma'am." The bachelor hung his head in false embarrassment. "I fear I was thinking of an entirely different sort of unspeakable."

A gurgle of laughter escaped Colly, but she pressed her lips together to control it. "Sir, while the unspeakable remains, thankfully, unspoken, I will leave you to contemplate your narrow escape."

"But, ma'am, surely you will allow me to—"

She covered her ears to let him know she was not listening; then she walked to the door. "You will be pleased to know, sir, that our good Wexler has sent someone to Canterbury to apprise your relative of your safety and, if possible, to bring you some fresh clothes to replace the ones so badly torn when you were injured. Tomorrow, if you have regained your strength, perhaps you will be able to rid yourself of the liability of your borrowed peacock plumes."

"Permit me to remind you," he said when she lowered her hands from her ears, "that fine feathers make—"

She closed the door before he could finish the platitude. Once out of his sight, she closed her eyes and breathed a sigh of relief. *All is well.* Her little white lie about being in love with someone had been inspired, and with the help of that revelation, it had needed only Ethan's easy manners to enable them to scrape through what she had feared would be a most mortifying encounter.

As she continued down the hall to the main stairway and then proceeded to the small dining room, where Miss Montrose and a nuncheon awaited her, Colly recalled that Ethan had always enjoyed a reputation for the smoothness of his address. "And he has not changed a bit," she muttered, a smile once again curving her lips.

If Miss Montrose noticed that her niece's thoughts seemed to be otherwhere during the meal, or that the distracted young lady's eyes betrayed a gleam of suppressed amusement when nothing in the least amusing had been said, she was too sensible a woman to question the cause of those unusual occurrences. After all, she reasoned, why ask questions whose answers the veriest nincompoop could have guessed?

Ethan napped longer than he had expected, and when he awoke, the sunshine that had warmed the room during the morning hours had given way to cooling shade; telling him that the day was well into afternoon. He felt both fresher and stronger after his nap. All traces of his headache were gone, and only an occasional throb reminded him of his injured shoulder.

With nothing else to do, he lay in the bed mulling over all that had happened since he had received his brother's letter four days ago. As this amusement palled within a short span of time, however, he began to think of himself as a neglected man. "A man could survive his injuries and die of boredom around here," he said to the room at large.

After another ten minutes of counting the muted silver stripes in the wallpaper, Ethan sat up and swung his muscular legs over the side of the bed. "Be demmed if I need to lie here like some invalid. Only my shoulder is injured; there is nothing wrong with the rest of me."

Tossing back the covers, he rose from the bed without any apparent ill effects, but after less than a dozen steps across the room, he discovered that he was weaker than he had supposed. His knees wobbled, almost buckling, and he was forced to grab a table to keep from falling. He did not fall, but a lamp did, with a loud thud.

Within seconds Miss Sommes threw open the door.

"Well," he said, a crooked grin on his face, "if I had known it was that easy to get attention around here, I would have knocked the lamp over thirty minutes ago."

Despite his bravado he held fast to the table. A thin line of perspiration appeared above his lip.

Colly stared at him, uncertain what she should do. He stood before her clad only in Sir Wilfred's dressing gown, a garment intended for a much smaller man, and his well-developed calves and portions of his muscular chest were fully exposed to her view. She had never seen a gentleman *en dishabille* before. The sight of any man only half clad would have been an unnerving experience for her, but the sight of a man of Ethan's exemplary fitness was doubly so. Her eyes had a will of their own. She could not seem to make them obey her command to look away.

She hesitated for only a moment. Then without a word of remonstrance for his foolishness, she walked over and put her arm around his waist. "Lean upon me, Lord Raymond, and perhaps we can contrive to return you to your bed without destroying any more of the furniture than is absolutely necessary."

Ethan obeyed without a murmur, placing his arm around Colly's shoulders and letting her lead him back to bed. When he was safely under the covers and his color had returned to normal, she smiled at him. "You surprised me, sir, with your acquiescence. I would have expected some argument from you."

A devilish smile lit Ethan's face. "Ma'am, I never argue with a lady who has just invited me to put my arms around her."

Colly felt her face grow warm. "Lord Raymond," she said with what she hoped was a quelling tone, "I begin to suspect that you are a seasoned flirt."

He was all mock seriousness. "Oh, no, ma'am. Not a seasoned flirt . . . a raw one, green as grass. A *seasoned* flirt would have gotten a kiss out of you to go with the hug."

Colly tried valiantly to keep a straight face but found the task beyond her. "Ethan Bradford, you are a cad!"

He donned the face of a penitent. "I know, ma'am. Do you suppose there is any hope for me?"

"None whatsoever!" she said with finality. "Now,

sir, if you will be serious for a moment, I came to your room for a purpose."

"Miss Sommes!" he admonished, feigning surprise, "how can you call me a cad in one breath, then get my hopes up in the next?"

Colly spoke slowly and dampingly. "Lord Raymond, did anyone ever tell you that you are a thoroughly disreputable person?"

"Yes, ma'am, numerous times." His face was forlorn. "But it never hurt my feelings until you said it."

She almost choked trying to suppress her laughter. "In just ten seconds," she threatened, "I am leaving this room. If you would like some tea, which is the question I came in here to ask, you had better say so now."

"I would love some tea." He gave her a slow smile that made her pulse quicken. "Especially if you will take pity on a lonely man and share it with me."

His softly spoken invitation, plus that smile, made it difficult for Colly to breathe. Unable to speak, she gave him a curt nod. Then she exited the room with what she hoped was not unseemly haste.

When the door clicked shut behind her, Ethan relaxed against the pillows, his good arm behind his head and a smile on his lips. He looked forward to a cup of bracing tea, but more to the point, he looked forward to Miss Sommes' return. He found her quick wit and her easy, unaffected manners surprisingly refreshing.

His brother, he decided, was a complete idiot! After managing, somehow, to convince a superior woman such as Miss Sommes to accept his hand,

Reggie was a fool to cry off. She would have made a most welcome addition to the Bradford family. With that thought Ethan's smile suddenly vanished. For some reason he didn't wish to examine, the picture of Miss Sommes in the role of his sister-in-law spoiled his good mood.

Twenty minutes later, his outlook brightened considerably when the object of his thoughts reentered his room accompanied by a maid who carried the promised tea tray and Wexler, who carried a lacquered wood chess board.

"Hallelujah! Chess. The very thing we need."

The board was actually a table fashioned with folding legs and a drawer that held the chess pieces, so while the maid poured the steaming tea and brought Ethan a cup and a plate of hot scones dripping with fresh butter, Wexler straightened the table legs and put the chessboard as close to the bed as possible.

"While you drink your tea," Colly said, "I will set up the pieces. And you had better eat a few of those scones while you are at it," she instructed saucily, "for you will need your strength. I am reputed to be an accomplished player."

Ethan gave her a measuring look while obediently devouring one of the crusty scones. "So, you are an accomplished player, are you?" He licked his lips, then reached for his teacup. "Just how accomplished?"

Colly blew upon her fingernails, then buffed them

against the Norwich shawl draped across her shoulders. "One hesitates to boast, sir, one really does."

"Oh, does one? And would you care to back that non-boast with a small wager, Miss Brass Face?"

Colly was momentarily taken aback by this plain speaking, but upon second thought she decided she preferred plain speaking to the usual inane conversation proscribed by society as proper between a man and a woman. After all, high sticklers for propriety would say she should not even be in a gentleman's room—be he ever so injured and the door ever so firmly propped open.

She decided to ignore the high sticklers. Ethan would not be here much longer, and it was too foolish for words to let an over-niceness of propriety rob her of this opportunity to enjoy the company of a charming, personable man. Furthermore, she was not some schoolroom miss whose every move must be chaperoned.

Her decision made to enjoy the moment, Colly cocked her head and peered at him saucily. "A wager, you said, sir. I fear I did not bring my reticule with me. Will my IOU suffice until after the game?"

Ethan inclined his head politely. "Certainly, ma'am. We are all gentlemen here, so to speak."

The game, whose stake was a shilling, lasted more than an hour. After the first five minutes Ethan knew he was pitted against a worthy opponent. The lady's moves were both considered and assured, and it required all his concentration and skill to guard his king. Nonetheless, his initial inattentiveness lost him the first game.

"You are beaten, sir!" Miss Sommes crowed, buffing her nails again and laughing. "I warned you how it would be." She held out her hand, palm upward. "Play and pay, my lord, play and pay. My shilling, if you please."

Ethan reached forward with his much larger hand and curled her outstretched hand into a fist, holding it fast. "A quite unsportsmanlike gesture, ma'am. A gentleman must always be allowed an opportunity to recoup his losses." He looked deeply into her laughing eyes, enchanted by the way the silver threads in her shawl drew out the gray in her eyes, and it was only when she slipped her soft hand from his that he realized he had held hers overlong.

"And another thing," he added quickly before she withdrew herself as well as her hand, "a true Corinthian, having won the game, would try for a little humility. He would never carry on in that most unseemly manner."

The lady took umbrage, as he had hoped she would. "I was not unseemly."

"I fear the truth hurts, ma'am." He began resetting the board. "Did your father never teach you how to be a good winner?"

She lifted her chin. "I am a female, Lord Raymond; gentlemen—even doting fathers—never expect a female to win at anything. Therefore, such Corinthian lessons as winner's humility never occur to those who instruct young females. I am, however, a most gracious loser. That lesson was thought to be appropriate . . . along with the ladylike art of dissembling and eyelash batting."

As if to demonstrate, she waved her hand beneath her chin as though it were a fan and batted her eyelashes at him. "Lah, Lord Raymond," she simpered, "I cannot think how a bird wit such as myself came to win out over a gentleman of your naturally superior skill, knowledge, and perspicacity. I wish you may not have taken a disgust of me."

"Too late," he said.

She abandoned her fanning and placed her fingertips over her lips to stifle her laughter. Ethan gazed at those fingertips as they pressed against her smiling lips and knew a strong desire to replace them with his mouth.

He was deterred from acting upon this totally inappropriate notion when Miss Sommes adjured him to take his first move. He did as he was bidden, and after an hour in which both combatants played their best, he was finally able to announce, "Check and mate."

Miss Sommes looked the board over for several moments before tipping her king over in capitulation. "This time I will honestly bow to your superior strategy, Eth—er, Lord Raymond."

"Thank you, ma'am. And please, I would be honored if you would call me Ethan."

She lowered her gaze, concentrating more than was necessary on the task of fitting the chess pieces back into the drawer beneath the table. "I would not dream of using your name, sir."

"And why ever not?" he asked, admiring the graceful curve of her neck and recalling the way she had looked when he first saw her: her glorious hair loose and tumbled about shoulders.

"Because, sir, *that* would not be seemly."

"Ha! After the Cheltenham drama you enacted earlier, batting your lashes and simpering like some bread and butter miss, I marvel that you have the audacity to utter the word *seemly*. Furthermore," he added, "you have already used my name."

"I never!"

"I hesitate to contradict a lady, but you did. It happened earlier this very afternoon. It was just after you called me a seasoned flirt, but before you referred to me as a disreputable fellow. You said, 'Ethan Bradford, you are a cad.' I remember it perfectly."

She looked as though she would like to deny his words but could not.

"So," he said, pushing home his advantage, "since you have already gotten into the habit, so to speak, you might just as well continue."

Colly stood up and began folding under the legs of the chessboard. When she had folded the last leg into place, Ethan reached out and caught her hand. His strong fingers curled gently around hers. "Please," he said softly. "All my friends call me Ethan."

For an endless moment Colly stared at his hand holding hers; then she lifted her gaze to his face. Not immune to the appeal in his brown eyes—so warm, so friendly—she concluded that it would be churlish to deny his simple request. "As you wish," she said. "But I warn you up front, Ethan, I never answer to Columbine."

Ethan drew her captured hand up to his lips for the briefest of seconds. "Thank you, Miss Colly."

The feel of his warm lips on her skin robbed Colly of breath, and she snatched her hand away in some confusion. "I must hurry and dress for dinner," she said, wanting to distance herself from this mesmerizing man as quickly as possible. "The gong will be sounding any minute now, and Aunt Pet will be obliged to wait for me."

Thinking she might have appeared abrupt, Colly turned when she reached the doorway and asked Ethan if he would like her to send up a book or two from the library.

"No," he said pathetically, a starved-dog look on his face, "not send. Bring."

Colly experienced that shortness of breath again, but she managed to speak evenly. "Sir, you are fast becoming a spoiled patient."

If possible, he looked even more pathetic. "I know, ma'am, and it shames me to reflect upon it."

"Balderdash!" she exclaimed inelegantly.

Colly could still hear his laughter as she closed the door behind her.

Chapter 5

The next morning Lord Raymond felt completely restored and announced his intention of quitting his sickbed. After having been shaved, then assisted into a coat of blue superfine by the servant who had brought his luggage from his elderly relative's house in Canterbury, Ethan slipped his arm back into its sling and declared himself ready to join the ladies below stairs.

Since the house was of respectable size rather than sprawling, Ethan had no trouble finding his way from the guest wing. He followed the wide, curving staircase down to the main floor, then crossed the polished parquetry of the hall to the morning room, where the two ladies had sat the day he arrived. With no servant in sight, he knocked on the door and waited to be invited to enter.

Miss Petunia Montrose bade him come in, but was obviously surprised that it was he who opened the door. After hastily adjusting the very fetching cap that matched the Bruges lace trim of her rose nainsook morning dress, she graciously extended her hand. "Do come in, Lord Raymond. I had no notion that you meant to quit your bed this morning. I trust you are feeling more the thing."

Ethan bowed over the older lady's hand, but could not restrain himself from glancing around the room. Miss Montrose was the only inhabitant. "Where is everyone?" he asked before he could stop himself.

"Everyone, Lord Raymond?" A look of speculation crossed the lady's face. "Do you mean everyone in general or perhaps one person in particular?"

Ethan silently cursed his stupidity. He had dodged enough matchmaking mamas to know that glint in a lady's eye. "Ma'am, in my youth I served as a lieutenant in the Hussars. And as any soldier will tell you, lieutenants must always be interested in the general."

"*Touché,* my lord." Smiling, Miss Montrose patted the sofa cushion, inviting Ethan to be seated.

"Thank you, ma'am."

He had only just settled his long legs in front of him when the French doors opened and Colly stepped inside the room. Though Ethan stood politely at her entrance, she did not at first notice him, so he availed himself of the opportunity to observe her for longer than was altogether polite.

Today she wore a pale green walking dress that still retained the black trim of mourning, and a small, shallow-crowned bonnet tied with black ribbons. Even allowing for the touches of mourning in her costume, her freshness put Ethan in mind of a wildflower. A smile came unbidden to his lips as he noted the touch of pink her walk had brought to her cheeks, and the smell of the clean, July air and sunshine that clung to her person.

"There you are," Miss Montrose remarked. "Lord Raymond and I were just wondering where you could be."

Colly turned a questioning glance toward her relative, but that lady had suddenly discovered a speck of dust on her lace-trimmed sleeve and kept her eyes downcast. Receiving no response from her aunt, Colly turned her gaze upon Ethan, who made her an elegant bow.

"I am surprised to see you among us this morning, sir. Are you certain you are strong enough to leave your bed?"

"Do I look so very pulled to you then, ma'am?"

"Oh, no, my lord," she replied with an innocent air, "it is only that we have so many lamps in this room. I would scarce know which one to grab if you were to swoon again."

Ethan acknowledged this sally with his eyes, but said aloud, "I am persuaded you have me confused with some other guest."

"No, sir. I am never confused about—"

"But do not be embarrassed by your mental lapse," he interrupted, "for I promise you that *I* shan't give it another thought. I believe I may even know its source. You have been walking, and it is my understanding that exercise often leaves young ladies with their wits gone begging."

"Ethan Bradford! Of all the unhandsome things—"

"But let us return to the question of lamps. If you truly fear for the safety of your crystal, the solution is within your power. You may give me a tour of the garden, if Miss Montrose has no objection, for I am woefully tired of being indoors."

Colly found nothing to dislike in this suggestion, and judging from the moonstruck expression on Miss Montrose's face, neither did that maiden lady. Suddenly wishing to quit the room before her aunt gave voice to any of the romantic notions that were written plainly upon her countenance, Colly grabbed Ethan's good arm and tugged the nature lover through the French doors and out onto the terrace.

The Sommes Grange garden was a well-tended yet unpretentious bower bordered on three sides by a hedge more than eight feet tall and almost as thick. Anyone inside the confines of that hedge could be seen only from the terrace. The privacy factor, as well as the fact that the hedge shielded the garden from the winter winds, made it a popular spot with the Grange inhabitants.

Ethan looked around him. The garden's privacy perfectly suited his purposes, as he had decided late last evening that he must delay no longer the business for which he had come to Sommes Grange. A carriage had been sent for him, and he could no longer impose upon the hospitality of the house. He must leave today. Before he left, however, he needed to speak with Colly about his brother's change of heart—and, of course, ask her to return the Bradford Diamond.

Finding the task even more distasteful now than it had seemed before he became acquainted with Colly, he let himself be distracted by his surroundings. "That small pink flower smells delightful," he said as they strolled down the brick footpath. "Do you know its name?"

"It is *Silene acaulis,*" she informed him. "Or moss campion, as it is commonly called in its native habitat."

At his bidding she named each of the flowers and border plants they passed, giving him the Latin as well as the common names.

"Your Latin is impressive, Miss Colly. On your lips it sounds like a real language, not that dull stuff we slogged through at Eton."

"I enjoy languages."

"In the plural?" He raised his eyebrows in mock surprise. "Don't tell me there are blue stockings beneath that green dress."

Colly shook her head. "I speak German and French, sir, but nothing to stigmatize me as blue."

"What? No Spanish? No Italian?"

"Perhaps a little Italian and a mere smattering of Spanish, but before I am cast quite beyond the pale, pray let me assure you that my geography is shaky, I find sums a dead bore, and I could not name a trade wind if it blew me down. Furthermore, I am addicted to sentimental poetry, and I adore novels from the Minerva Press—the ghastlier, the better."

Ethan's laughter disturbed a thrush, which deserted a low stone bench for the safety of the hedge top. "I acquit you of all suspicion, Miss Colly. While a bluestocking might admit to reading sentimental poetry, she would certainly draw the line at owning up to a taste for trashy novels."

He pointed at the stone bench vacated by the thrush. "Perhaps you would care to stop for a while and regale me with a lurid scene or two from one of those marble-board treatises."

"Are you tired, Ethan? By all means, let us sit down if you are fatigued. Pray do not overtax yourself on your first day out."

"I feel perfectly fit, I assure you," he said, then added much too casually, "I thought perhaps you might feel the need to rest."

"I? And why should I feel the need to rest? I have not sustained an injury."

"Oh, I know that, ma'am. I was remembering your advanced age. Nearing twenty-five, I believe you said."

At first she resolved not to dignify his absurd remark, but a disobedient chuckle betrayed her into a retort. "Sir, you are a cad and a bounder for throwing all my confessions back at me!"

"Very true. And it would serve me right if you never wore that dress again."

"And now what maggot have you got into your head?"

Ethan waited until she was seated, then disposed himself beside her, turning so he could watch her face. It was a truly beautiful face, he decided. "Do you have any idea what that green dress does to your eyes?"

She shook her head, rendered speechless not so

much by the personal turn of the conversation as by his softly spoken words.

"As we walked from sunlight into shade, then back into sunlight, the green of your dress caused your eyes to change color. They went from a sparkling green to a soft, mysterious grey, then returned once again to sparkling green." His next words were almost inaudible. "A most alluring phenomenon."

The unexpected gallantry sent Colly's pulse racing. Was Ethan setting up a flirtation with her? Unable to discern the answer to that question, and not wishing to appear gauche by saying the wrong thing, she folded her hands in her lap, giving her full attention to her laced fingers.

Neither of them spoke for a time. As the silence stretched between them, broken only by the thin, reedy notes of the thrush, Ethan slipped his arm from its sling and took both her hands in his. "I shall be returning to Canterbury today, Miss Colly, but before I go there is something I must say to you. I am afraid I can delay it no longer."

At a loss as to how she should respond, Colly looked up into his face. To her surprise, the humor that usually lit his eyes was gone, their expression was completely serious. "I am listening, Ethan."

"What I have to say pertains to your plans for the future."

Something like a warning bell went off in Colly's brain. Her future? Surely he did not mean . . . She took a deep breath. Could Ethan possibly be trying to fix his interest with her? She tried to still the sudden thumping of her heart.

"Miss Colly, though I have known you for only a short time, I feel as though we have become friends. I admire you, and I wish with all my heart that I could shield you from sorrow. I wish it were within my power to—"

Shield her from sorrow? Colly felt as if her lungs were being constricted by one of those old-fashioned whalebone corsets. Ethan Bradford was about to make her an offer! She tried to concentrate on his words, but the gentle pressure of his hands upon hers made that nearly impossible.

". . . then yesterday," she heard him say, "when you confided in me that your affections were engaged, I knew that—" Whatever Ethan knew, he was stopped from revealing it to her, interrupted by the sound of footsteps on the brick walk.

"Ethan!" called a plump, red-haired gentleman Colly had never seen before. "Are you all right, dear boy?"

"Winny! What the deuce are you doing here?"

A full thirty minutes passed before Ethan received an answer to his question. First he presented Mr. Harrison to Colly; then after the introductions were made, good manners dictated that they return to the house to exchange a few minutes of polite conversation with Miss Montrose. Only after the amenities were observed could Ethan beg to be excused for a private word with his old friend.

"Demmed fine-looking lady," Mr. Harrison remarked as soon as the book room door closed behind them. "Seems intelligent, too. Difficult to believe she would have anything in common with that brother of yours."

Not really expecting a reply, the newcomer plopped into one of the two upholstered chairs the cozy room boasted and got right to the question uppermost in his mind. "Since you and Miss Sommes seem to be on easy terms with each other, I can only assume that she took the news of Reggie's perfidy with equanimity. Was it equally easy to reclaim the Bradford Diamond?"

"Never mind about the ring, Winny, I have everything in hand on that score. What I want to know is what the devil brought you here."

"A cursed rented hack, that's what. Worst bag of bones I ever threw a leg over, but preferable to last evening's mail, which is how I traveled to Canterbury."

"I meant *why* are you here? What on earth possessed you to leave town?"

"Not what, dear boy . . . who. It was Lady Raymond."

"What has my mother got to do with—"

"She is at Raymond House. And you will not credit the bee she has got in her bonnet."

Ethan sat down in the chair opposite his friend. "Did she find out about Reggie's engagement?"

"No. Not but what it would have been better if she had. But it ain't my place to poke my nose in your family business, so I'll keep my tongue between my teeth. Anyway, Reggie's name never came up."

"Then why is she in town?"

"Seems Lady Raymond decided to have some jewelry cleaned before the season started, and that is when she discovered the Bradford Diamond missing. Naturally, she assumed you took it."

"A reasonable assumption. But I see no reason why that should send her to town."

"Looking for you, dear boy. Chased me to earth yesterday afternoon. Then before I knew what was afoot, she wormed it out of me that you had come to Canterbury."

"And?"

"She planned to leave town this morning, so I took the mail last night to get here before her. Thought it only right that I warn you, considering all the scrapes you pulled me out of when we were lads at school. Not that I ever figured out why all those bullies seemed bent on drawing my cork, but still I—"

"Cut line, Winny! Warn me about what?"

"Told you Lady Raymond had a bee in her bonnet. She put two and two together and came up with five. Your mother is coming to Canterbury, dear boy, to meet the future baroness. Plans to make herself known to your fiancée."

"Kind of your aunt to invite us to nuncheon, Miss Sommes, but I must say I wish we weren't leaving so soon. Wish there was time to get to know you better."

Colly stared at the visitor. Though his countenance showed unmistakable signs of habitual affability, she was surprised at this show of interest from a gentleman she'd met less than an hour earlier.

They were in the morning room alone, having arrived there before Ethan and Miss Montrose. While Mr. Harrison leaned against the mantel, sipping a glass of sherry, Colly sat on the yellow silk sofa where she could observe the door without appearing to do so. Schooling her features to display a calm she was far from feeling, she watched for Ethan. She hoped for a sign from him that he wished to continue the surprising, though not unwelcome, conversation interrupted by Mr. Harrison's untimely arrival.

"Perhaps we shall meet again soon, sir. My sister makes her bow at the queen's next drawing room, and I will be in town later for her ball. I will ask my mother to send cards to both you and Lord Raymond." When she pronounced Ethan's name, her voice trembled slightly, as the thought occurred to her that by the time of the ball, she might be his betrothed.

"Kind of you to invite us, ma'am. Beg a dance from you, if I may."

"Of course, sir."

Mr. Harrison set his glass on the mantel and walked over to sit in the chair nearest Colly. "Ma'am, Ethan and I have been friends since we were boys, and I do not believe I can leave here without telling you how much I admire the way you have handled this entire affair. I must say, you are a most remarkable lady."

Colly felt herself blush with annoyance at his fulsome compliment. Surely he did not refer to their having cared for Ethan after he was injured. Did he think they would toss an injured man onto his horse and send him back to Canterbury? "You pay me too much tribute, sir. One does the best one can in any situation."

"Just so, ma'am. And I am certain I speak for Ethan as well as myself when I say that any family would be proud to welcome a lady such as yourself into their fold."

Colly felt the heat rush to her face again. Had Ethan told this man that he meant to make her a declaration?

"Of course," the gentleman continued, "the lad is young yet. Much too young to become a tenant for life."

Too young? Was Mr. Harrison making sport of her? Ethan was thirty, old enough for matrimony by anyone's standards.

"Be that as it may, the young scamp had absolutely no right to take the Bradford Diamond. The ring belongs to Ethan."

Colly glanced at the sherry bottle to see if Mr. Harrison had dipped into it more than she knew, but even as she did so, something he said began to niggle at her memory. He spoke of a ring. Ethan had mentioned a ring the day he arrived at the Grange. At that time, of course, she had been too stunned by his sudden appearance to pay close attention to anything he said. And before he had been there above a

half-dozen minutes, they were interrupted by the unfortunate arrival of her papa's stallion.

While Mr. Harrison droned on, Colly tried to recall what Ethan had said the day he arrived. He said
he had some business to discuss with her; she remembered that now. Then, for no apparent reason,
he had mentioned a ring. She also remembered him
asking her if she was acquainted with his brother.
No, not asking, accusing. If she remembered correctly, his tone had been most uncivil.

Mr. Harrison chuckled, reclaiming her attention.
"So when Reggie sent that letter saying you and he
were engaged, Ethan decided he had better come
down here to straighten out the affair."

Colly gasped. *Engaged!* What was he saying?

The speaker smiled benignly at her. "No need to
be concerned, ma'am. Ethan burned the letter, so no
one else saw it. Of course, the dear boy had no idea
when he bolted down to Canterbury that he would
meet a lovely lady like yourself. Just goes to show,
does it not?"

Colly felt as though she were living a bad dream.
Why would this Reggie person—someone she had
never met—claim to be engaged to her? And just
what kind of female had Ethan expected to find here
at the Grange?

"If you can believe it, Miss Sommes, we did not
even know your full name. All Ethan had to go on
was your last name. His brother has such deplorable
handwriting that Ethan and I both thought the lad

was engaged to someone named Milly, or perhaps Gilly."

Gilly! Colly felt the hand of fate knock the breath from her. Gilly. Of course. She might have known that madcap would land them all in a bramble bush the moment she got away from home. But surely even Gilly wouldn't be so careless of her chances for future happiness as to enter into a clandestine engagement.

Of course she would! Her sister did whatever popped into her beautiful head, and she was forever fancying herself in love with one fellow or another. Young men had begun falling in love with Gilly even before she left the schoolroom.

But what was their mama thinking of not to keep a closer watch on the girl? Had neither of them any idea what a scandal a clandestine engagement would cause?

Colly closed her eyes as sudden embarrassment warmed her face. Mama and Gilly might be unaware of the potential scandal, but Ethan Bradford, the sixth Baron Raymond, was not.

It all made sense now. Ethan's sudden arrival. His anger. He had come to Sommes Grange to end the engagement of his younger brother to a female of possibly questionable background. And by mischance—a slip of the pen—he thought *she* was the object of his brother's affection.

Colly pressed her fingernails into the soft flesh of her palms to make herself remain calm. She had never questioned Ethan's reason for coming to her home. If she were honest with herself, she would admit that she was too pleased to see him to question anything. Now questions chased one another through her brain: questions about Ethan's gallantry, his marked attention toward her, his protestations of friendship. Were they all just an act meant to turn her up sweet? Were they the weapons he had used to keep her from causing a scandal that would embarrass his family?

Mortification almost choked her. Colly had been such an easy prey to Ethan's charm. How besotted she must have appeared earlier in the garden. Like some love-starved old maid, she had let him cozen her with sweet talk about the color of her eyes. She had even convinced herself that he was about to offer her his hand and his heart, when all the time he was merely trying to rescind his brother's offer.

What a fool she had been. She wanted to scream at her own gullibility. The Lord Raymonds of this world did not marry the daughters of obscure country gentlemen. Nor did they bestow their younger brothers on those obscure misses. Colly had known that all along, yet she had let herself believe that Ethan found her as fascinating and desirable as she found him.

A tightness obstructed her throat. She felt a gnawing emptiness in her stomach that had nothing to do with the delayed nuncheon.

"Forgive my tardiness," Aunt Pet said, entering the room on Ethan's arm.

"And mine," Ethan added, his handsome face warmed by a smile and his eyes alight with what

Colly might once have believed was a look meant only for her.

After Ethan declined her aunt's offer of sherry, Colly allowed Mr. Harrison to lead her into the dining room. While that loquacious gentleman beguiled Aunt Pet with all the latest *on dits* about the royal dukes and their prospective brides, Colly's anger boiled. She took no part in the conversation but kept her attention focused on her plate.

At some point talk of the royal nuptials was abandoned, and the conversation turned to the subject of the Montrose family names.

"Yes," Aunt Pet said, "all the Montrose females are named for flowers. My father's mother was called Iris, and his sister was named Columbine. Our Colly was named for my Aunt Columbine."

Aunt Pet smiled at her, and both gentlemen did the same. Colly did not return their smiles. It was almost more than she could do to remain at the table with Ethan now that she knew what a fool he had made of her. She willed this meal to end so that he would leave the Grange and she might never have to look at him again.

"My brother upheld the tradition," Aunt Pet continued, "by naming Colly's mother Violet. And, of course, my nieces are Columbine and—ouch!"

After a brief glance at Colly, Miss Montrose composed herself and did not acknowledge by word or gesture that she had just been ruthlessly kicked in the shin. She saw the message of distress in her niece's eyes, nodded her receipt of that message, then turned the conversation to the flowers in the Sommes Grange garden.

Colly breathed a sigh of relief. She did not want Ethan to discover the true identity of his brother's fiancée. At least not until she had had time to talk with her sister and do what she could to salvage that flibbertigibbet's reputation. Ethan's interests lay with his family's good name, and though she acquitted him of any wish to hurt her own family, she could not be certain that he would not rush to London and try the same tactics on Gilly that he had tried on her.

Her sister must be warned. She did not possess Colly's level head. Gilly might be swayed by Ethan's handsome face and charming manners, by that way he had of looking deep into a woman's eyes—making her feel as though he saw into her very soul. Colly felt a lead weight somewhere in the region of her heart.

The meal finally ended, and while the carriage that had been sent for Ethan's use was summoned, as well as his horse and the bone rattler Mr. Harrison had ridden, Ethan asked Colly if he might have a private word with her.

This time she cherished no girlish illusions about his reasons for wishing a private interview. With her head held high, and her face revealing none of the emotions she felt, Colly led him to the book room. Once inside, she rudely remained standing, thereby forcing him to do likewise.

"Miss Colly, there is something I must tell you before I leave. I wish I had not to say it. Believe me, I do not relish the thought of giving you pain, but—"

"Just say it, Lord Raymond, and let us have done."

Ethan stared, puzzled by the coolness of her tone. If not for the fact that they parted only an hour ago on the best of terms, he might have thought she was angry with him. He decided he must have misheard her.

When he attempted to take her hand, however, she moved around to the far side of the desk letting the furniture act as a buffer between them. He tried to look into her eyes to see if she was teasing him, but she turned away, giving her full attention to the perusal of an aged ink spill on the desk blotter.

"Miss Colly?" he asked softly, "have I said or done something to give offense? If so, I assure you I—"

"I believe I hear your carriage, Lord Raymond. If you have something to say to me, delay it no longer."

Ethan could not reconcile the coolness in her voice with the friendly banter they had enjoyed such a short time ago in the garden. "Miss Colly . . . Colly, please tell me what has you—"

"My lord, if you have something to say to me, then say it. For I have every intention of quitting this room in exactly one minute."

Ethan knew her well enough to know she meant what she said, so he took a breath and spoke the words he had been dreading for the last two days. "It grieves me to be the bearer of news that will, I fear, distress you. But my brother has asked me to ask you if you will consent to release him from his commitment to you."

"As you will," Colly replied, still giving the ink spot her full attention. "Your brother is hereby released. And now, Lord Raymond, as you have accomplished that purpose for which you came to Sommes Grange, I believe your carriage awaits you outside."

Many times Ethan had imagined this scene, and in each instance he had pictured Colly either collapsing in tears or bearing the news in brave, though stunned silence. He was unprepared for her anger, her undisguised contempt. It bothered him more than he wished to admit. "Colly," he said softly, "I know this news is upsetting to you, but if you will let me explain how—"

"My feelings can be of no interest to you, Lord Raymond, just as your explanations are of no interest to me."

Ethan reached across the desk and playfully tugged the tendril of hair that rested enchantingly against her cheek. "Colly, please do not kill the messenger. I thought we were friends."

"One must always be on guard against self-deception, Lord Raymond." She caught the curl he had tugged and ruthlessly shoved it behind her ear. "And now, my lord, since we have nothing more to discuss, you may go. You need not trouble yourself to take leave of my aunt."

He heard her in dismay. Colly was dismissing him as though he were a servant! He would not have believed she could act so churlish. After all, this had been almost as unpleasant for him as it was for her;

surely she could see that. As she continued to stare at that spot on the desk blotter, her silence attesting to her anger, Ethan felt his own temper begin to rise.

"I am afraid I cannot go just yet," he said. "There is one more thing we must discuss. The betrothal ring."

Colly looked up so quickly he could almost believe the subject surprised her. "The betrothal ring?"

"If it was not a family piece, I am certain my brother would wish you to keep it. But under the circumstances . . . " He let his words trail off, still wishing to give as little offense as possible.

A *family piece!* Colly felt her knees grow weak and threaten to give way beneath her. She labored valiantly to maintain some semblance of composure. An heirloom. Drat Ethan's brother for giving Gilly an heirloom, and drat her sister for accepting it. Naturally Ethan would expect her to return an heirloom. She searched for some reasonable excuse for not being able to return the ring, but could think of nothing.

The silence stretched between them. She could tell Ethan was only just controlling his irritation with her.

"Since you obviously find my continued presence distasteful, Miss Sommes, if you will send a servant for the ring, I will bid you good day and take myself off."

Deciding her only hope was to bluff her way through this latest development, Colly squared her shoulders and made her tone offhand. "I do not have the ring, my lord."

"What do you mean, you do not have it? Where is it?"

She raised her shoulders ever so slightly. "I cannot say at this time. Perhaps I left it in town. I will send a note to my mother. If she finds the ring, she can have it sent around to your London house."

"If? *If* she finds it? Madam, we are speaking of the Bradford Diamond!"

"Then by all means, let us hope she finds it."

Ethan's eyes were glacial. "Let us hope so indeed!"

Colly swallowed, wishing she was anywhere but in this room, uttering words that sank her deeper and deeper into deceit.

"It would be most embarrassing," Ethan said, his words clipped, "if I should have to sue for the ring's return."

"Sue!" Colly felt her own temper flare again. This was the outside of enough. "You would threaten me thus? Have a care, Lord Raymond, for you are putting some rather interesting ideas into my head. You might be surprised to discover that two can play at that game. I wonder how embarrassed your family would be if I should decide to bring suit against your brother for breach of promise."

Chapter 6

"Aunt Pet, have you ever seen the Bradford Diamond?"

"Oh, yes. That is to say, not in person, of course, but I did see a drawing of it in a book on historical jewelry. A magnificent gem, so the book said. Brought back from the Crusades, I believe."

Colly pushed aside the heavy curtain and stared out the inn window into the bustling courtyard. Owing to its prime situation just off the main Canterbury road, the posting inn was always busy, but Colly noticed none of the activity going on outside. No matter how hard she tried, she could think of nothing but the unpleasant scene she had had with Ethan that afternoon before he left the Grange. How very angry he had been when he stormed out of the book room.

Of course, she had been angry, too. And hurt.

Not that she had anyone but herself to blame for the latter emotion. She had thought of nothing else all afternoon, and honesty forced her to admit that

perhaps she had read too much into what passed between Ethan and herself during his convalescence.

In retrospect she saw that she had made her first
mistake by allowing the relaxation of the proprieties.
The degree of familiarity between them had led—no,
misled—her into reviving an old dream, an impossible dream she had packed away with her presenta-
tion gown seven years ago. In all fairness to Ethan,
she could not recall the slightest hint from him that
he wished to turn her dream into a reality.

Colly shook her head in disbelief at her own flight
of fancy. She had been foolish beyond permission. In
a mere two days' time she had let her thoughts leap
from an exchange of mutually enjoyable banter to an
exchange of wedding vows. How lowering to discover
that she was as deplorably romantic as Aunt Pet.
And I cautioned Ethan about self-deception!

These self-recriminations were interrupted by
Miss Montrose, who, whole of heart, was enjoying a
light repast at a small table drawn up to a comfortable wing chair. "I begin to think the girl has forgotten about the tea you requested, my dear. Are you
certain I cannot tempt you with a bit of this ham? It
is delicious, I assure you."

Placing another slice of the wafer-thin ham on her
own plate, the lady continued, "The mail coach will
be here within the hour, Colly, and I have it on good
authority from the innkeeper that once we board the
coach, we will find little opportunity for decent sus-
tenance until we reach London. And though I quite
agree with you that we must reach town with all

haste, I see no reason why we need do so on empty stomachs."

Colly crossed the garishly patterned carpet that covered the floor of the small private parlor and returned to the stiff upholstered chair she had only recently vacated. When her aunt served her a slice of ham, she picked up a fork and idly pushed at the meat, never once lifting it from the plate. "Is it very beautiful?"

"The mail coach?" asked her astonished aunt.

"The Bradford Diamond."

"Oh, the diamond. I suppose it must be beautiful; only think of its value, its history. Though to tell the truth, it put me in mind of nothing so much as a glass doorknob. Consider the drawbacks of being obliged to wear such a large stone, for it must catch one's shawls and snag one's stockings dreadfully, not to mention absolutely ruining one's gloves."

The maiden lady paused, letting the hand that held the serving spoon remain suspended midway between her plate and a dish of creamed onions, a bemused expression on her gently lined face. "Of course, I daresay one would overlook the stone's disadvantages if one were a young lady in love with the ring's owner."

The sigh that followed this observation reminded Colly that she had promised to accompany her romantic aunt to Canterbury to see the German princess and her aging swain, the Duke of Clarence. Now, of course, there would be no time for watching the royals; Colly must get to Gilly before that foolish damsel made the mistake of broadcasting her betrothal. Even leaving by post this evening, they could hope to reach London no sooner than early tomorrow morning.

Colly reached across the table and squeezed her aunt's hand. "Forgive me for spoiling your plans."

"Nonsense, my dear. I could not let you go to London alone, not in a public conveyance. Besides, I—"

The door opened and the maid bustled in, her plain, round face red with excitement. "I be that sorry, miss, about your tea." She set the small tray down next to Colly's plate. "The place is all sixes and sevens, you might say, on account of the German princess. Mr. Gaines is all yelling and ordering, he is, and his rib is in the kitchen threatening a fit of the vapors, what with her not being used to cooking for royalty."

Miss Montrose's eyes lit with excitement. "Never tell me the Princess Adelaide is to stop here."

"Lah, ma'am. Already here, she is. Come just after I brung in your dinner, she did. With her ma—the duchess, the gentlemen as is escorting them called her—and two others as must be ladies in waiting. Not that anyone here knows for sure what they are," she added with a touch of scorn, "them not speaking the king's English and all."

"German is their native tongue," Colly reproved gently. "Are we to despise them for speaking the language of their birth?"

"Germans," the maid said, ignoring the reproof by rolling her eyes heavenward. "Always marrying Germans. First our dear Princess Charlotte—God rest her soul—now all her uncles. Can't none of them find any but Germans to marry, they can't."

"If no one speaks English," Aunt Pet said to get the conversation away from the popular grievance and back to the subject of the princess's party, "how were they able to make their wishes known?"

"The two gentlemen as escorted them here made all the arrangements. Even ordered a fire in the ladies' rooms, they did—and it July. The ladies went t'rectly to their rooms. Worn out, I guess they were. Then the gentlemen drove to another inn."

"Only think of it, Colly. The princess. In this very inn. How exciting it is, to be sure." Caring not a whit that she was gossiping with a servant, Miss Montrose turned once again to the maid. "Did you see her—the princess, I mean? Was she handsome?"

"Lah, ma'am, old Gaines catch the likes of me standing around gawking at the guests, he'd have my hide, he would. But Bess, as took their hot water cans up, said the princess was slender. A blond lady. Pale like, so Bess said, and looking pulled, probably from the long sea voyage."

Suddenly catching the sound of her employer's raised voice on the other side of the door, the girl bobbed a quick curtsy and hurried from the room. Unfortunately, the door did not catch fast behind her, and it slowly swung open. Almost immediately Colly and Miss Montrose heard the voices in the hallway.

"I'm that sorry, ma'am," Mr. Gaines said with such

stentorian loudness they could not help overhearing, "but I've no notion what it is you be a-wanting."

Colly heard only a few words of the speaker's soft reply, but they were enough to tell her the words were spoken in German. Without giving it a second thought, she rose from the table and went to the door. "May I be of help, Mr. Gaines?"

The beleaguered innkeeper turned hopeful eyes toward her. "Miss Sommes. I'm that sorry to disturb you, miss, but if you can help, I'd be much obliged. This lady seems to want something pretty bad. Only thing is, with me not being one as knows foreign tongues, I got no notion what that something is."

He turned back to the lady and raised his voice, as though volume alone might breach the language barrier. "Tell this here lady what it is you be a-wanting, ma'am."

Colly stepped out into the hallway and smiled politely at the dark-haired woman. "*Entschuldigen, Sie. Bitte, kann ich Sie haelfen?*"

"*Danke schon,*" replied the lady, the relief in her eyes matching the relief in her voice. "*Danke schon, gnadige Frau.*"

"Ethan," his mama declared, patting the neat silver-streaked coiffure only that moment arranged by her abigail, "you are an annoying creature, and I wish you would not vex me in this odious manner. After I have traveled all the way to Canterbury, then been forced to spend the better part of the afternoon listening to my cousin Theodosia and her parsimonious ranting about overfed servants, pray do not let my efforts go unrewarded."

"It grieves me to disoblige you, Mama, but I cannot introduce you to a female who does not exist. I have not bestowed the betrothal ring upon anyone, as you will see in a matter of days when the ring is returned to the vault, cleaned and with the loose mountings secured."

"Gammon! You must think me a slowtop."

"Acquit me, ma'am. I know you to be awake on every suit."

"And I know Spanish coin when I hear it!"

Lady Raymond dismissed her maid; once she was alone with her son, she looked down the straight nose that was the feminine counterpart of Ethan's own appendage. "You put me out of all patience, Ethan. You were always one to keep your own counsel, but this time it will not serve. I have come to make the acquaintance of my future daughter-in-law, and I will not be satisfied until that objective is accomplished."

"Upon my honor, ma'am, there is no such person."

After several moments of silence Lady Raymond removed a wisp of lace from inside the sash of her mauve wrapper and pressed it to the corners of her dark eyes. "You know it is my dearest wish that you find a suitable *parti*. And by 'suitable' I do not mean just some pretty widgeon who can fill your nursery. You must choose someone capable of filling your heart as well. Someone who—" Her voice broke, forcing her to swallow before she continued. "One who will make you as happy as your dear father made me.'

Ethan lifted the lady's plump fingers to his lips. "And as you made him, my dear."

Lady Raymond laid her free hand on her son's broad shoulder for a brief moment. Then she yanked her fingers from his grasp and bade him return to his chair and quit trying to turn her head with sentimental reminiscences. "For I will not be thwarted in this. I must, and will, meet Miss Sommes. I wish to see for myself if she is the right gel for you. I want no *marriage de convenance*. Not for either of my sons."

Short of telling her the truth about her youngest son's latest debacle, Ethan could not convince his mother that he was not himself secretly betrothed. Finally, when the gong sounded, warning the household that it was time to dress for dinner, he made a grateful exit from his mother's room.

Back in the musty-smelling room assigned to him, Ethan dropped into a sagging wing chair and stretched his feet out before him on the threadbare Turkey carpet. Angrily he yanked the pristine cravat from around his neck and threw it toward the empty fireplace. "Women!" he muttered.

At that moment he would have given half his estate for a decanter of *anything*. Unfortunately, his elderly cousin's notion of hospitality did not extend to providing her guests with refreshments in their rooms, especially strong drink. Resigning himself to the situation, Ethan leaned his head back against the chair and closed his eyes.

Two unpleasant interviews in one day were too much! First Colly, then his mother. And though the interview with his mother had not been as difficult as he had feared, it was no pleasant thing to dissemble to someone he held in esteem.

As to the argument with Colly . . . he did not even want to think about that *contretemps*. Not it, or her.

Without even realizing he was doing so, Ethan reached inside his coat and removed the handkerchief he had put there earlier that day. Absently he placed the white linen on the arm of the chair, then unfolded it, revealing the infamous curl. The hint of lemon verbena that still clung to the silken tress toyed with his senses.

He had spent most of the afternoon trying to forget about Colly—forget how angry she had made him, and how he had longed to shake her until she recanted her threat to sue Reggie for breach of promise. Now, however, he realized that trying to forget her was an exercise in futility. With the scent that was so much a part of her filling his nostrils, his thoughts returned not to the angry woman in the book room but to the person he had come to know in the past two days.

Letting his memory travel where it would, Ethan recalled her intelligence, her quick wit, the light that sparkled in those mysterious gray-green eyes just before she burst into laughter. Thoughts of Colly's eyes led him to a contemplation of her lovely, serene face, and from there to the glorious hair he longed to loosen, as it had been the first time he saw her.

Almost against his will he lifted the light brown curl and slowly brushed it across his parted lips. The fragrance of her, the feel of her soft hair, reawakened the desire he had felt the previous evening—that desire to feel her full, satiny lips beneath his. Although now he admitted to himself that he had wanted more than just a taste of her sweet lips. Then, as now, he had wanted to crush her in his arms, to mold her tantalizing body against his, and to kiss her until she begged him to stop . . . or not to stop.

Someone scratched at the bedroom door, interrupting Ethan's musings, and without even asking himself why he did so, he carefully refolded the linen and returned the curl to the safety of his pocket. "Come in," he called.

A rather subdued Mr. Harrison peeped around the door. "It is only me, dear boy. Come to apologize. That is, if you ain't planning to give me the cut direct. Wouldn't blame you if you did, by Jove, not after me opening my budget to Miss Sommes this morning. Cannot tell you how sorry I am about—"

"Winny, you fool, come in and shut the door."

Mr. Harrison did as he was bidden, a look of relief on his face. "I heard you leave your mother's room. How is Lady Raymond?"

"Inquisitive. And unstoppable. I think the only course open to me is to return to London as quickly as possible and see if Colly's—that is to say, Miss Sommes'—mother can locate the ring. Not until my mother sees the diamond back in the vault will she believe that I am not indeed betrothed. Once I have returned the ring, she will cease to question me, and I can put this entire episode behind me for good and all. Then I can forget I ever laid eyes on the cursed woman."

Mr. Harrison had no difficulty discerning to which woman the epithet *cursed* was applied. Nor, for that matter, had he missed Ethan's use of Miss Sommes' given name—a most interesting slip of the tongue. But having already cast himself into the briars once that day, he decided to keep his own tongue between his teeth.

"You are fortunate," he said, watching Ethan's reaction closely, "that you *can* put it all behind you—give Miss Sommes your P.P.C., as it were. What I mean to say, no need to worry about her fate."

Ethan sat up, suddenly alert. "What the deuce are you talking about?"

"Just reassuring you that this episode will not blight her chances. Told you before, Miss Sommes is a fine-looking woman—devilish fine-looking. And with the entire town succumbing to marriage fever, I shouldn't be at all surprised to see the lady betrothed again before the end of the season."

The militant expression in Ethan's eyes at this prediction told Mr. Harrison all he wanted to know. Once again, however, he chose the wiser path of discretion and kept his observations to himself.

"Flaming coxcomb!" the scarlet-coated mail guard yelled at the coachman. "Now we be in the suds!

That wheel be broken clear through, you bacon-brained Jehu!"

Colly heard the angry words above the frantic stamping and neighing of the horses and the painful humming inside her head. She had been asleep when the coach started down the steep grade, but by the time it came to rest at its present dizzying angle, she had been thrown against the roof, the door, her aunt, and the roof again. At her final landing place —the debris-strewn floor—she had hit her head against the metal footrest.

"Colly, dear. Are you hurt?"

"Only a little, Aunt Pet. Were you injured?"

"Bruised but unbroken. I was not asleep when the vehicle went out of control, so I managed to hang onto the strap and avoid being tossed about too severely. Let me help you up, dear."

Pushing aside a small carry case, two bonnets, and a dog-eared copy of Maria Edgeworth's *Vivian*—all of which had fallen on her niece—Miss Montrose put her hand beneath Colly's arm and helped her up off the floor.

"Idgit!" yelled the guard. "Couldn't let a body get out and secure the skidpan. No. Not you. You got to puff off how strong you are . . . how you can make the wheel horses hold on any hill. Bah! Now see what you gone and done, you great looby!"

Very cautiously, Colly touched the back of her head, fingering a bump that had already begun to swell. "I am a bit fuzzy still, Aunt. What happened?"

"It would appear that our driver—yon *idgit*— rather overestimated his driving capabilities and has now run us into a ditch. I collect that the rear wheel is broken."

"Quit your jawing, Mr. Know-it-all!" the coachman retaliated. "Shut your gabber and get down and help me with the horses. And you," he ordered the ashen-faced passenger who still clung to the sides of his rooftop seat, "jump down and see if you can help the inside passengers; there's a good lad."

Within seconds the door was wrenched open, and a young man with a thatch of unruly blond hair poked his head inside the coach. "Anyone hurt?"

"I am merely shaken," Miss Montrose replied, "but my niece has sustained a knock on the head. Be so good as to help us to alight, for the tilt of the coach is making her decidedly unwell."

There was no mending the wheel, so less than an hour later, when the first signs of dawn began to lighten the sky, the guard secured the mailbags to one of the coach horses and galloped off down the road. His first obligation was the delivery of the mail, but he promised to send help to the stranded coach as soon as he reached the next town.

Quite soon after the guard's departure, Colly decided she preferred the discomfort of the tilting coach to the greater discomfort of the morning dew, which was rapidly soaking her from head to toe. At her aunt's ready agreement, the two ladies crawled back inside the coach, where, with the help of a shared lap robe, they made themselves as comfortable as possible while waiting for daylight and, hopefully, a speedy rescue.

The rescue came by mid-morning, for which Miss

Montrose and her niece expressed their gratitude. Unfortunately, their rescuer was the last person in the kingdom Colly wished to see.

The sun had been up for several hours, and both the dew and Colly's headache had very nearly evaporated. Hoping the fresh air would blow away the few cobwebs that remained inside her head, Colly had decided to take a short excursion into a nearby meadow full of young hay and wildflowers.

With her apple-green Kerseymere already bedraggled from the night spent in the coach, she gave little thought to the further damage done the traveling dress or her kid half boots by the damp earth of the meadow. It was only when she pushed her way back through the hedge of Queen Anne's lace and foxglove that separated the meadow from the road that she regretted having added to her disheveled appearance.

A handsome traveling chaise and four had stopped to offer assistance, and standing beside the vehicle was a tall, broad-shouldered gentleman dressed in a beautifully cut Devonshire brown coat, neat biscuit-colored trousers, and top boots whose shine rivaled the sun. And though he stood a good twenty yards away from Colly and faced in the opposite direction, she recognized him on the instant. It was Ethan.

Her initial reaction was one of embarrassment that Ethan should catch her looking like a hoyden, with her shoes muddied and her skirt damp and wrinkled. Fast on the heels of that reaction, however—and far more unnerving to Colly's continued peace—was the traitorous excitement that leapt inside her chest at the very sight of him, no matter what the circumstance.

Almost as if he heard her wildly beating heart, Ethan turned and looked directly at her. "Colly!" he said, shock written all over his handsome face. "Never tell me that you were in that accident. Are you inj—"

"By Jove!" Mr. Harrison interrupted, stepping down from the chaise and unwittingly blocking his friend's view of the stranded lady. "A pleasure to see you again so soon, ma'am." Smiling, the newcomer removed his curly brim beaver, then approached Colly as though he had encountered her strolling through Hyde Park instead of crawling through a hedge along the Rochester road.

Her face warm with embarrassment, Colly hurriedly dumped the mass of yellow snapdragons and blue cornflowers she carried in her bonnet, then set the now damp straw on her windblown curls. "Sir, I . . ."

As though unaware of her dishevelment, Mr. Harrison bent over Colly's hand in an elegant manner. "Ma'am," he said. Then, with an amused light in his eye, and as wicked a smile as Colly had ever seen, he admonished his friend to come see who he had found. "For I grant you will be as surprised as I am, dear boy. Here is Miss Sommes."

Despite the elegance of Lord Raymond's well-sprung traveling chaise, Colly would remember the final leg of her trip to London as the most miserable three hours of her life. After the postilion transferred their luggage from the boot of the mail coach to Lord Raymond's equipage, Mr. Harrison gallantly assisted Colly and her aunt into the chaise, then took his place on the opposite seat. Instead of climbing in behind his friend, however, Ethan declared his intention of riding up top with the driver. "To give the ladies more room," he said.

Colly did not believe him. Not for a moment. It was obvious to her that Ethan could not abide the thought of spending several hours in her company. His innate chivalry would not allow him to leave them stranded on the road, but it could not alter the fact that he was still very angry with her—angry because he believed her to be the kind of unprincipled woman who would become engaged to a boy and then refuse to return a valuable family ring once the betrothal had ended.

Under the circumstances, she could hardly fault him for his anger. Unfortunately, she could say nothing to disabuse him of the misconception, not without betraying her sister.

Colly felt the coach rock as Ethan climbed up top. Moments later the coachman cracked his whip and the horses sprang into action. For a reason she did not wish to examine, her headache returned, and with it an uncomfortable tightness in her chest. The sway of the coach—back and forth, back and forth—only added to her misery, reminding her of couples waltzing in each other's arms.

Her fellow travelers seemed to notice neither her distress nor Ethan's unusual behavior. On the contrary, they appeared quite pleased to be in one another's company, chatting companionably and smiling on occasion, almost as if they shared some interesting secret to which Colly was not privy.

"The Princess Adelaide and her mother stayed at the same inn we patronized yesterday," Miss Montrose offered, abandoning their polite discussion of the state of the roads for a subject much more to her liking.

"By Jove. Thought I saw a pair of familiar coaches as we were leaving Canterbury. Told Ethan they reminded me of a pair I had seen used by the royal princesses." The gentleman toyed absently with a gold fob and chain that hung from the pocket of his beige-and-moss striped vest, the lids of his slightly protuberant eyes half closed in speculation. "So, the duke's betrothed has arrived at last, has she? Clarence was there to meet her, I suppose."

"Actually, no—that is to say, if the Duke of Clarence was in attendance, *I* did not see him."

"Didn't come, eh? Very unloverlike, to be sure. But then Clarence does not possess his brother's address with the fair sex. Must be planning to meet the princess in town." Mr. Harrison smiled. "Placed a small wager regarding the length of their betrothal. Be interesting to see firsthand what develops."

"Oh, yes," Miss Montrose agreed with a dreamy sigh, blissfully unaware that her companion, far from sharing her wishes that the engagement progress rapidly to a royal wedding, actually had wagered on its dissolvement within a specified number of days. "My niece spoke to one of the party," the romantic lady continued, "the Duchess Eleanor's lady-in-waiting, I believe she was."

"You don't say. Would not have supposed any of them could speak the king's English."

"Oh, they did not," Miss Montrose informed him. "Colly spoke to the lady in German."

"By Jove!" the gentleman said, his eyebrows raised in half-moons of surprise. "Ethan said Miss Sommes was an intelligent young woman, but . . . well, I mean to say, *German!*"

Colly had ceased listening to the conversation inside the chaise several minutes earlier, more interested in the gentleman who sat on the roof of the conveyance than in Mr. Harrison's speculations upon the betrothal of the royal couple; therefore, she missed the fact that Ethan had been discussing her with his friend. Unaware of this interesting piece of information, she let her thoughts drift back to the day Ethan had arrived at Sommes Grange, and to the days that followed. Days, she realized now, that had changed her life.

Until Ethan came to Sommes Grange, she had been reasonably satisfied. Naturally, there had been a few private moments when she acknowledged that there was a void in her life, but her deep-seated aversion to loveless marriages kept her from making too much of that void. Until Ethan came.

Not that she had been unhappy, she reminded herself. She had her family, a number of enjoyable companions in the neighborhood, and her charitable work at the Sunday school. But after Ethan came, she began to feel the need for something more in her life. Or perhaps *someone* in her life.

Colly closed her eyes and leaned her head against the squabs. She was deluding herself again, unwilling to admit the truth, for the truth, once acknowledged, must be dealt with. It was not an unknown "someone" Colly wanted in her life, it was Ethan. She loved him. Honesty made her admit it, if only to herself. She was in love with Ethan Bradford. She had loved him seven years ago, and she loved him even more today.

The Pandora's box of honesty now open, she asked herself how she could love a man who despised her—a man who could not even bring himself to ride in the same carriage with her. The answer was simple: she could not control her heart. But, she vowed, she could control her actions. She would not make a cake of herself by wearing her heart on her sleeve. Nor would she allow herself to become an object of ridicule, the latest *on dit*.

Ethan did not love her. Never mind that she loved him; he despised her. All he wanted from her was the return of the Bradford Diamond. Since she knew how he felt, all she could do was find the ring, return it to him, tell him good-bye, then take herself back to Sommes Grange.

It was a good plan—she knew that. And it was the right thing to do—she knew that also. The only thing she did not know, could not even imagine, was how she would live the rest of her life knowing she would never see Ethan again.

Chapter 7

Lady Sommes and Gilly had put up at Grillon's Hotel at number 7, Albermarle Street for the duration of their current stay in town. Sir Wilfred would, of course, rent a suitable house for Gilly's come-out, but for this three-week orgy of visits to the modistes for fittings, plus trips to the various linen draper's shops for gloves, stockings, fans, and such fripperies, a suite at Grillon's answered the ladies' needs quite tolerably.

Since the primary purpose of Gilly's and Violet's trip was shopping, Colly was not surprised to find them absent when she and Miss Montrose were ushered into the suite. However, when she discovered that the abigail they were sharing for the trip was also not in evidence, Colly began to question where they were.

"I shall see what I can discover," Miss Montrose offered. "While I make the inquiries, my dear, I wish you would go to your sister's room and lie down upon her bed, for I am persuaded that you continue to suffer somewhat from the accident."

"But, I—"

"Please. No buts. From the moment we entered Lord Raymond's chaise, you uttered scarcely a word, and I know you would not have behaved so very ungraciously if something were not amiss. Nor, after his lordship was so particularly kind as to stop at that inn at Farbury and procure a private room for us in which to refresh ourselves, would you have refused all but the veriest mouthful of the lovely collation we were served. I can think of no other reason for such exceedingly rag-mannered behavior except that your head continues to distress you."

Colly blushed; the scold was both legitimate and deserved. "I am sorry if I embarrassed you, Aunt Pet."

"Think no more about it," declared the lady, patting her niece's cheek. "Depend upon it, it is nothing more than a case of the headache. Come now, you had much better lie down until it disappears completely."

Unwilling to disabuse her aunt of the assumption that it was a pain in her head, rather than an ache in her heart, that had her in such low spirits, Colly agreed to lie down for a time. "After I am rested," she offered, "I shall pen a note to Mr. Harrison begging his pardon for my lack of social graces and expressing my appreciation for his many kindnesses."

Miss Montrose's tone was studiedly uninquisitive. "And what of Lord Raymond? Shall you write to him as well?"

Feeling the heat rise again to her face, Colly turned and walked toward the bedroom to the left of

the small sitting room. "I shall write to Lord Raymond when I return the Bradford Diamond. I am
persuaded that he will find one letter sufficient for
both offices."

After she closed the bedroom door, she lay down
upon the satin-covered tent bed, where she remained for less than a half hour. She was unable to
rest. Having raised the subject of the Bradford Diamond again, she could not erase it from her mind.
Finally, unable to wait another moment for her sister's return, she rose from the bed and crossed the
room to the dressing table, where she looked for
Gilly's jewelry box. She found nothing there beneath
a small looking glass except a number of carelessly
strewn *fol lols*.

A thorough investigation of the dressing table
drawers also revealed nothing. The drawers of the
mahogany chiffonier proved even messier than
those of the dressing table, but similarly unfruitful.
Only after an exhaustive search of the nightstand, a
half dozen bandboxes from the modiste's, three reti-
cules, several pairs of shoes, and the bracket clock
on the mantel did Colly surrender to the inescap-
able: The Bradford Diamond was not in Gilly's room.

As Colly looked about her for any hiding place she
had missed, an idea occurred to her—an idea she
would not have credited earlier, not even to her foolish sister. "Gilly, you dolt," she muttered, "you must
be wearing the ring."

Horrified at her own words, she turned and ran to
the sitting room. "Aunt Pet!"

Miss Montrose had only that moment returned to

the suite, followed by one of the hotel maids and a footman pushing a loaded tea cart. Spying the servants, Colly forced herself to remain quiet until the footman bowed himself out of the room and the maid was dispatched to Lady Sommes' bedroom to see to the unpacking of Miss Montrose's clothes.

"The ring is not here," Colly said as soon as they were alone.

"Not here? Then where—"

"Gilly must be wearing it. The little fool!"

Her aunt concurred completely with Colly's assessment of this supposed lack of good judgment on Gilly's part, but far from soothing Colly, Miss Montrose's agreement only increased her uneasiness. And as her agitation grew, Colly seemed to lose her usual quickness of perception, failing to question the wisdom of her aunt's next, rather impassioned suggestion.

"We must find the silly child," Miss Montrose declared. "Tonight! We must wrest the ring from her finger! For her own good, of course," she added more sedately.

"But, Aunt, we do not know where she is."

"As to that," Miss Montrose replied, her eyes not quite meeting those of her niece, "someone or other of the staff—I cannot at the moment recall who it was —informed me that Gilly and Violet were promised to attend Lady Sedgewick's musicale this evening. They probably were promised some place for dinner before the musicale and have planned to go straight from that other place to Lady Sedgewick's. We will find the foolish chit there. Hurry and drink your tea, my dear, and do try a few of those jam tarts. We will not wish to be late."

Colly blinked. "Late? For what? Surely you do not mean that we should go to the musicale?"

"But of course. We have no other choice if we are to find your sister before she commits some further impropriety."

Colly could only stare at her aunt. "But we have no invitation."

"Pshaw. A mere trifle, I assure you. I have known Aurelia Kent these thirty years and more, and she is seldom acquainted with above half the people who attend her parties. Furthermore, with town still a bit thin of company, she will most likely fall upon our necks with gratitude for filling out the empty chairs."

"Be that as it may, we have nothing suitable to wear to a musi—"

"*I* brought a suitable gown. As for you, your mother's room is filled with bandboxes; there must be at least one gown among the clutter that would serve. I know better than to suggest one of Gilly's new purchases, for all of her come-out gowns will be white, and white has never done you justice."

"Dear me, no," Colly shuddered, remembering the whites that had been de rigueur when she made her own miserably lackluster come-out seven years ago. Added to the impediment of her crushing shyness had been the certain knowledge that she had looked quite insipid in the required white. "No," she said quietly, "not one of Gilly's gowns."

Less than two hours later, elegantly attired in a deceptively simple gown of jonquil silk that was ruched at the shoulders and hem and banded in deep gold, Colly found herself among a small throng of people making their way up the marble staircase of an impressive Grosvenor Square town house. Still uncertain how she had come to agree to such rash behavior, she kept her eyes downcast, fearful that at any moment the butler would denounce her as the interloper she was and have her escorted from the premises.

Her nerve almost deserted her when it became her turn to shake hands with their hostess, a purple-turbaned matron whom Aunt Pet addressed blithely as "My dearest, dearest Aurelia."

Not by so much as a raised eyebrow did Lady Sedgewick betray her total inability to recognize Miss Montrose. With a half smile her ladyship mumbled some name that might have been anything from Anne to Zantibe, then saluted her visitor's wrinkled cheek with a light kiss. Shaking Colly's hand, their hostess assured them both that she was most pleased they had been able to join her little musicale.

Letting go the breath she held, Colly captured her aunt by the arm and hurried her toward a columned archway that gave access to a spacious blue and silver music room. "Let us find my sister quickly," she whispered, "so that we may leave this place. I still cannot like being here under false pretenses."

"But, my dear, I assure you—"

"And," she warned, "before you perjure your immortal soul even further with that flummery about your lengthy acquaintance with Lady Sedgewick, allow me to inform you that I do not believe for one mo—"

"Miss Montrose! Well met."

"Why, Mr. Harrison," the lady replied happily, pulling her arm from Colly's grasp and extending her hand to the gentleman as though it had been three years since their last meeting rather than slightly less than three hours. "What a delightful surprise, to be sure."

Deprived of all speech, as well as manners, by the unexpected appearance of Mr. Harrison, Colly quickly scanned the room to see if he had come to the party alone. To her dismay, he had not. She missed the conspiratorial look that passed between Mr. Harrison and her aunt, because at that moment she had eyes only for a tall, dark-haired man who stood across the room amid a group of animated young gentlemen.

The sight of Lord Raymond—unbelievably handsome in a black evening coat, white waistcoat, snug pantaloons, and flawlessly arranged cravat—made her knees grow week, obliging her to rest her gloved hand against the fluted column of the archway to maintain her balance. Colly had always subscribed to the canon that a gentleman ought to be as handsome as he could, but observing Ethan at that particular moment, she bemoaned the unfairness of his taking the principle and turning it into a weapon.

While Colly struggled to regain her composure, Ethan lifted his gaze, and though an entire room divided them, he looked directly into her eyes. The smile he had worn a moment earlier faded. When the laughing gentleman at his elbow spoke to him, Ethan bent his head politely to listen to the remark, but he continued to stare at Colly. She scarcely knew what to make of that intense expression in his eyes; it seemed to rob the room of all breathable air.

From what seemed a long way off, she heard Miss Montrose speak her name. "Colly, my dear, Mr. Harrison asked you a question."

By superhuman effort she forced her attention away from the compelling brown eyes that still held hers. "I beg your pardon, Mr. Harrison."

"Asked your preference, Miss Sommes."

"Preference? I am afraid I do not underst—"

"Mr. Harrison wishes to know if you have a preference as to seating, my dear. Lady Sedgewick is signaling for the program to begin."

Too disconcerted to remember that they had come to the party for only one purpose—to find her sister—Colly agreed that Mr. Harrison should select whatever spot he thought most convenient. To her dismay, the gentleman escorted them to chairs at the top of the long room, very nearly close enough to touch the pianoforte. Colly realized an instant too late that the prominence of the selected seats prevented them from escaping the room before the entire program was completed. And to add to her dilemma, she discovered that her chair was only one chair removed from that of her heretofore unknown hostess.

A hostage by forfeit of her own ability to command her senses, Colly determined that if she could not actually be calm, she must at least strive to appear so.

By the time the first soloist had completed his trilogy of tenor ariosos, she had succeeded in her objective and schooled her face to its usual serenity. She might even have maintained that pose if she had not turned slightly to her left and discovered the ornate, gold-framed looking glass that hung between the two floor-to-ceiling windows. Clearly reflected in the looking glass was the ruggedly handsome profile of Ethan Bradford, the sixth Baron Raymond.

Colly looked away immediately. However, after she worked it out in her mind that Ethan was unaware of his reflected image—due to the angles of the room—she allowed herself another peek at the glass. He had not taken a chair but stood in the archway, his shoulder resting against one of the fluted columns, and from the sober expression on his face, the rather dramatic duet of harp and pianoforte gave him little pleasure.

Colly had no idea what it was that led her to the conclusion that Ethan's attention was caught not by the duet but by her. Intuition perhaps? Whatever it was, the moment she thought it, she knew it was true: All the while she had been watching his reflection in the glass, he had been watching her. She felt her face grow uncomfortably warm, and only by the strongest exertion of willpower was she able to remain in her chair.

She felt Ethan's eyes upon her during the remainder of the program. Throughout the interminable

performances of art songs, lieder, and concerto—
some quite good, others rather ordinary—Colly
never again peeked at the looking glass. But she
knew if she had, she would have found Ethan still
watching her.

As soon as the last smattering of applause faded
away, gentlemen began offering ladies their escort
down to supper. Mr. Harrison proffered both his
arms. "Miss Montrose, Miss Sommes. May I have
the pleasure?"

"No!" Colly answered quickly before her aunt
could reply in the positive. "That is . . . thank you,
sir, but I fear my headache has reappeared. I must
return to the hotel."

The next day being the Sabbath, the two ladies at-
tended services, then returned to the hotel; at which
time Colly discovered from the concierge that Gilly
and Lady Sommes had repaired to the country for a
few days. "As I told Miss Montrose when she in-
quired yesterday," added that worthy.

"So you did, my good man," replied the maiden
lady. Then, discovering a heretofore unnoticed snag
in her favorite reticule, she was able to concentrate
on that misfortune and thereby avoid the accusing
look aimed her way by her exasperated niece. "When
one is overtired from a long journey," she said, "one
is apt to mishear a message."

"True," Colly agreed, her tone ironic. "An honest
mistake. The concierge said, 'Country,' and you

heard, 'Lady Sedgewick's musicale.' It could happen to anyone."

"Yes, indeed. Anyone."

With no wish to discuss the previous evening, Colly let the subject drop, whereupon her grateful aunt suggested they procure a light nuncheon, then go for a short stroll.

Following the stroll, they spent the remainder of the day in quiet conversation and reading. That is to say, one of the ladies read. Colly's book lay open upon her lap, but the words on the page could not compete with the images that interfered with her concentration. Images of a pair of warm brown eyes and a mouth that had at one time worn a ready smile. Thankfully, the long day finally came to a close, and Colly was free to retire to her bedchamber, where she tossed and turned for hours, still plagued by those same brown eyes and the smile that had turned to anger.

The next morning, Miss Montrose opened the door to her niece's room and exclaimed cheerfully, "Time to get up, sleepyhead. Wake up, do, for you have slept the clock around. It wants but twenty minutes until ten of the clock, and so many exciting things have happened while you lay abed."

"Must I?" mumbled Colly.

Tugging at the cover her niece tried to pull over her head, Miss Montrose said, "Here is the maid with your tray. Sit up, there's a good girl, and drink your chocolate while I tell you about my morning."

While the maid yanked aside the curtains to let in the bright summer sunshine, Colly entertained the notion of turning her face into the pillow and begging for just ten minutes more. When she noticed the excitement on her aunt's face, however, she knew she could not do so. Stretching lazily, she pressed her fingertips against her eyelids to dispel the lingering traces of sleep.

In all truth, she had not slept the clock around but had lain awake until sunrise mulling over several disquieting questions—questions to which she had no reassuring answers. The first: Why had Ethan watched her all evening? The second query, and the one that had troubled her most: Was she doomed to spend the rest of her life haunted by the memory of a pair of brooding brown eyes?

"My dear," Aunt Pet said, reclaiming Colly's attention, "you will never guess who is here. Not here in this suite, of course, but staying at this hotel, at Grillon's."

"I have no—"

"The Princess Adelaide," she answered before Colly could offer a conjecture.

"Surely not, Aunt. The princess has traveled all the way from Germany to marry a royal duke; it would be thoughtless beyond permission to put her up in a hotel. I am persuaded she must be at Kew with the queen."

"Thoughtless or no, the princess is here at this hotel. I was downstairs in the ladies' reading room, perusing this month's *Repository of Arts*, when suddenly I heard German being spoken nearby. You may imagine my surprise when I looked up to discover the lady you assisted at the inn in Canterbury

—the one for whom you procured a hot tisane to soothe her *mal de mer*. She stood just outside the reading room, discoursing quietly with a distinguished-looking gentleman who I assumed must be one of Princess Adelaide's escorts."

Colly sat up and reached for the cup of hot chocolate and a slice of toast. "And did you see the princess?" she mumbled between hungry bites.

Miss Montrose shook her head. "Alas, I was not so fortunate. But I shall see her; I have determined upon it! Since I cannot trust fate to be forever putting the princess in my way, I have chosen a chair in the ladies' reading room, one that offers a good view of the foyer and the grand staircase, and I have ever intention of taking up residence in that chair. I shall remain at that spot until I am allowed at least a glimpse of the young lady who may one day be our queen."

Colly finished the last of the toast and licked her buttery fingers. "If I can be of assistance, Aunt Pet, you have only to ask. After all, I did promise something of the sort in Canterbury."

Miss Montrose's face was a study in innocence. "How glad I am that you recalled your promise to me, my dear, for I have been worrying this hour and more over what to do about Mr. Harrison."

"Mr. Harrison? What has he to say to anything? If you desire to watch for the princess, it is none of his affair."

"But the young man wished to show me his new curricle, and ever mindful of the debt we owe him for delivering us safely to town, I agreed to an outing." Her aunt smiled beatifically. "Thank you for solving my problem, my dear. Now I can watch for Princess Adelaide, while you accompany Mr. Harrison to the park in my stead."

Colly almost choked on her chocolate. "Aunt Pet! I cannot go for curricle rides in the park. Especially not with Mr. Harrison."

"Of course you can," her aunt replied. "Especially since it is with Mr. Harrison. Allowing him to drive you about will save you having to write a note of apology for your rudeness yesterday." She let that piece of logic do its work before she continued. "For my part, I cannot think it too much to ask that you repay the gentleman's kindness to us by admiring his new equipage. Young men like that sort of thing, don't you know? And," she added as a clincher, "fresh air always puts you in such good looks."

Though Colly put forth any number of arguments as to why she should not accompany Mr. Harrison in his new curricle, Aunt Pet would not be dissuaded. Finally, buckling under the pressure of the pledge she had made to her aunt and the debt she owed Mr. Harrison, Colly agreed to the outing.

Forty minutes later, fetchingly attired in one of Lady Sommes' new carriage dresses—a peach cambric with willow green volans on the sleeve and a similar flounce inside the V neckline—Colly opened the sitting room door to welcome Mr. Harrison. The smile she had summoned froze on her lips as she looked into the surprised face of Lord Raymond.

"My lord," she said weakly, "I was expecting Mr. Harrison."

"And I was expecting your aunt," Ethan replied. "Winny sent around a note saying he had forgotten a prior commitment, and asking me if I would drive Miss Montrose to Hyde Park. I am his proxy."

Colly felt an obstruction in her throat. "And I am my aunt's."

Because she was alone in the suite, there could be no question of her inviting a gentleman inside. Not that Colly wanted to do so, far from it, for she realized that if Ethan was invited inside he might justifiably ask her to search for the Bradford Diamond while he waited. Feeling a desperate desire to quit the premises as quickly as possible, she grabbed the parasol that matched her dress, informed her reluctant escort that she was ready for their drive, then brushed past him to step out into the hallway.

Ethan closed the door to the suite, then caught up with Colly at the top of the grand staircase. When he politely placed his hand beneath her elbow, he felt her jump nervously at his touch. He smiled. Far from being sympathetic to her embarrassment at being thrust into his company, it buoyed up his spirits. She deserved some kind of retribution for having fled the musicale last evening before he had time to show her how completely disinterested he was that she had come.

He was no less surprised than she at their being

thrown together today, but for reasons he did not wish to examine too closely, the thought of spending a sunny afternoon in her company did not displease him. Looking down at the lovely profile that peeked from beneath the abbreviated poke of her straw bonnet, he rationalized his feelings by acknowledging that no man with blood in his veins would refuse an opportunity to escort such a beautiful woman. And judging by the number of heads he saw turn as he led Colly through the hotel foyer, there were at least a dozen men in that very establishment who would be more than happy to exchange places with him.

The ride from Albemarle Street to the park was accomplished in complete silence, though the reasons for the silence varied considerably with the participants. While Lord Raymond gave his full attention to the spirited bays that pulled Mr. Harrison's curricle, Colly desperately searched her mind for an opening remark that would not remind her escort of the missing betrothal ring. She could think of nothing.

When Ethan tooled the bays through the south gate, Colly discovered the avenues of the refreshingly cool green park more congested than might have been expected on a July afternoon. Pleased by this circumstance, she prayed the heavy traffic might continue to occupy his attention, making conversation impossible. To her dismay, her prayer went unanswered.

"Are you comfortable?" Ethan asked as he deftly

maneuvered the curricle into the queue of phaetons and barouches that snaked its way along the road.

"Quite comfortable, my lord," she replied, feigning interest in a chestnut stallion being cantered down Rotten Row by a middle-aged horseman.

"Not too much sun, I trust."

She indicated the small parasol she held over her left shoulder. "I came prepared."

"Of course. Very pretty workmanship."

"You are very kind, sir."

Colly knew better than to hope they might beguile the entire ride with such innocuous remarks, for even though Ethan appeared relaxed—as though he had nothing on his mind save enjoying the drive—she could feel the pent-up energy emanating from him. It was almost, she thought, as if he were making a game of her, toying with her like some hapless prey. Did he enjoy keeping her off balance? she wondered. Was he planning to pounce upon her when she least suspected?

When their way was barred by a carriage that had come to a stop to allow its occupants to exchange greetings with the driver of a high-perch phaeton traveling in the opposite direction, Colly licked her suddenly dry lips, certain Ethan would seize the opportunity to demand once again the swift return of the Bradford Diamond.

"Miss Sommes," he began, shifting in the seat so he could face her, "I—"

"Raymond!" someone yelled. "I say there, Raymond, wait up."

As one, Colly and Ethan turned to observe the

middle-aged gentleman on the chestnut stallion gal-
loping toward them.

"The devil take it," Ethan muttered. Then, as the
gentleman drew near, "Good afternoon, Uncle."

"Ecod, Raymond," the gentleman began, "it is you.
I told myself it could not be so, yet here you are.
What on earth brings you up to town at this time of
year? I saw your mother a few minutes ago, but she
said nary a word about your being in town as well.
Not that you ain't welcome, of course. Always glad
to see you. I hear you mean to take your seat in Parliament—all that dreary school business, I suppose.
Waste of time and money, that. Why you must needs
involve yourself in something that has nothing to do
with you is more than I can understand. I remember
my own years at school. Beastly food and all that,
but still—"

"Monotonous food is the least of the problems be-
setting the parish schools," Ethan interrupted when
his uncle stopped for breath. "And I believe the
plight of London's children must ultimately affect us
all. But before we fall into a discussion that is best
left to other times and places, allow me to make
you known to Miss Sommes." He turned to Colly.
"Ma'am, my mother's twin brother, Mr. Philomen
Delacourt."

Though fascinated by this new picture of Ethan as
a man of social conscience, Colly remembered her
manners and inclined her head politely. "Mr. Delacourt."

"Servant, ma'am," he replied, lifting his hat. "I
say, did you call her Miss Sommes? I met a Lady

Sommes just t'other day. Handsome woman. Pretty
as a picture, actually, even if she is the mother of a
grown daughter. The daughter's a yellow-haired
chit. Can't remember what she called the gel—
some frippery name—but a positively breathtaking
child. Bringing the chit out during the little season, I believe. I daresay the gel will be a success.
Bound to break all the young men's hearts; won't
be able to help herself. Yes, positively breathtaking."

This time the gentleman seemed not to breathe at
all, leaving no room for appropriate responses from
his listeners. "You related to Lady Sommes, ma'am?
Of course, you must be. Handsome as you are,
obliged to be related. Can't hold a candle to the yellow-haired chit, of course, but you are still a handsome—"

"Uncle Philomen!" Ethan spoke angrily, surprising
Colly as well as his loquacious relative. Before either
of them had time to do more than stare, however,
the carriage that had delayed their progress moved
on.

Ethan touched the brim of his hat with his whip
handle. "Excuse me, Uncle, but I must not impede
traffic. Please stop by Raymond House later and take
tea with my mother." Having proffered his less than
cordial invitation, Ethan gave the bays their office
and moved ahead, leaving his uncle to stare after
him and think what he might.

Ethan looked beyond the horses' heads, focusing

on nothing in particular. *Cannot hold a candle, indeed. The old fool!* "My apologies," he said finally.

"For what, sir?"

"For my uncle. He was ever a rattle, but until today he has refrained from giving insult."

Colly studied Ethan's profile. Something in his tone—a sort of anger held in check—made her suspect that it was he who felt the insult. "Should I have been insulted? I assure you Mr. Delacourt said nothing to put me to the blush. Unless, of course, you think I should have taken exception to his comparing me to my sister."

Ethan glanced at her upturned face. "Do you not?"

Colly shook her head. "T'was no more than the truth, I assure you. No one can hold a candle to Gi—er, my sister. You may ask anyone in Canterbury or its environs. She is the most beautiful girl in the area."

"Impossible."

"Upon my honor, sir, it is the truth. You have not yet seen her."

"No," he said quietly, "but I have seen you."

Colly was surprised into silence by his words, afraid to take them for the compliment they sounded like. After all, she had deluded herself once before. Looking about her for something to say that would not reveal the effect his softly spoken words had upon her breathing, she spied the flower beds bordering the footpaths that meandered through the park. "I see my family is well represented in Hyde Park."

"Ma'am?"

She pointed at the fragrant blossoms, artfully laid out so that blankets of pink, blue, purple, white, and yellow were repeated every few feet. "See that white, showy group of flowers over there, the ones resembling a flock of doves? I blush to admit it, but those are my namesake, *Columbinus Aquilegia*. And growing next to the columbine you will notice a group of purple, funnel-shaped flowers, dignified yet unpretentious. Those, you will recollect, are *Petunia violacea*."

"I will recollect nothing of the kind, Miss Bluestocking. And I find it ungracious in you to make sport of my ignorance."

Ethan was smiling, and that teasing light Colly had thought never to see again shone in his eyes, reminding her of the fun they had shared not so many days ago. She felt her lips curve in response to his smile. "T'was merely a figure of speech, sir. I assure you I had no intention of—"

"Blast!" Ethan said, surprising his companion into silence. The smile he had worn only moments ago disappeared so quickly Colly wondered if it had been a figment of her imagination. She followed the direction of his gaze to an elegant silver-trimmed black barouche approaching from the opposite direction. The occupant of the carriage, a plump, middle-aged lady, hailed Ethan eagerly. His response was anything but eager as he reined in the bays once again.

"The Montrose family may be well represented in

the flower beds," he said, a note of resignation in his tone, "but mine seem to be annoyingly ubiquitous upon the roads."

"Sir?"

"My parent," he answered simply.

"Ethan," his mother greeted happily as their carriages pulled opposite each other. "How fortuitous. I did not think to meet you until dinnertime."

Though Colly was the last person Ethan wished to introduce to his parent at this time, the avid curiosity animating Lady Raymond's face convinced him that if he did not make the introductions, his mother might blurt out some ill-advised comment that would put them all to the blush.

"Mother, may I present Miss Columbine Sommes?"

"Did you say *Sommes?*"

Must all his relatives react in this surprised manner at the sound of her name? Though Ethan gave his mother what he hoped was a quelling look, at his nod of affirmation she breathed a sign of exquisite happiness.

"My dear, dear Miss Sommes. How delightful to make your acquaintance."

In the minutes that followed, Colly hardly knew how she should act. Lady Raymond, while being most cordial, exhibited an interest in her that was disquieting, to say the least. Like her ladyship's brother, Mr. Delacourt, Ethan's mother seldom stopped for breath, and with the thoroughness of a field marshal she questioned Colly about herself and the entire Sommes family. Following the interrogation, she paid Colly numerous compliments on her looks, her style, and her pretty manners.

But most unsettling of all, while she spoke, Lady Raymond continually employed a lace handkerchief, dabbing tears from the corners of her eyes. If Ethan had not insisted that only he and Mr. Harrison knew of the clandestine betrothal, Colly might almost have believed that Lady Raymond viewed her in the light of daughter-in-law elect.

To Colly's relief, the gentleman in the Tilbury directly behind the curricle called out to Ethan, wanting to know when he might expect to be allowed to continue his drive. With a hurried salute Ethan told his mother they would have to stop blocking the road.

"Of course," Lady Raymond agreed, smiling benignly at Colly. "One cannot have a decent conversation in the park these days. Miss Sommes, you and your aunt must join me this evening at the theater, where we may converse at our leisure. I have procured a box at the Haymarket."

"But—" Colly began.

"Please, Miss Sommes, I will not hear a negative reply."

Unable to think of an excuse that would not give offense, Colly asked if she might be allowed to check with her aunt, then send Lady Raymond her answer by one of the hotel footmen.

"An excellent idea," Lady Raymond agreed. "I hope to see you this evening." As her coachman signaled to his horses, Lady Raymond waved her sodden handkerchief at her son's vanishing curricle.

For several seconds Ethan looked straight ahead. Then, the tone in his voice a combination of exasperation and protectiveness, he said. "Would that my relatives were more like the flowers and less like a flock of chattering magpies. I apologize, Colly, for the catechism."

"Oh, no, really. I—"

"You need not feel obliged to attend the theater. I will explain to my mother that you have other plans."

While Ethan turned the bays toward the park gate, Colly concentrated on the trees and flowers, unable to look at him. She wondered if he had any idea how vulnerable he had sounded. When they had argued in the book room at Sommes Grange, she had thought him proud; she had assumed that he did not want his brother betrothed to her because he believed his family superior to hers. She questioned that assumption now. It was conceivable that Ethan had meant only to protect his brother from the folly of his actions, no matter who the lady involved. Perhaps he cared only that Reggie have a chance at future happiness. Colly could not fault Ethan for that; it was what she wished for her sister . . . and for herself.

As before, the drive on the busy streets was completed in silence. Only this time Colly felt none of the strain of the earlier trip, for she had come to a decision regarding the Bradford Diamond. Thanks in part to the meetings with Mr. Delacourt and Lady Raymond, Colly thought she had a clearer picture of

Ethan's character, and if he asked for the diamond
once they were back at the hotel, she would explain
the whole to him and trust to his good sense not to
let any gossip touch her sister's name. For her part,
Colly would like nothing better than to abandon this
role of the jilted lover, even if it prompted Ethan to
wring her neck for leading him on a wild goose
chase back to London.

As it transpired, Ethan did not ask about the diamond, Colly did not confess her subterfuge, and the
question of a throttling never arose. Though for
Colly's peace of mind, a throttling would have been
preferable to the near accident that, although
averted, resulted in an assault on her senses.

When Ethan reined in the bays at Grillon's, he
tossed the ribbons to the doorman, then went
around to assist Colly from the curricle. As he
started to reach his hand up to her, however, the
nervous bays shied, taking exception to the nearness
of an obstreperous pair being driven by a cow-
handed tulip in a high-perch phaeton, and at the
sudden movement of the curricle, Colly was pitched
forward.

Unable to find any handhold to save herself, and
thinking herself as good as beneath the treacherous
hooves of the frightened horses, Colly could not
credit her good fortune when a guardian angel of
surprising quickness crashed into her body, knock-
ing the air from her lungs and forcing her back onto
the safety of the curricle's box seat. As she struggled
for breath, her angel from heaven turned into a
being whose strong arms, muscular thighs, and

swearing masculinity were most definitely of this earth.

Curbing his angry oaths with obvious difficulty, Ethan slowly eased his body from atop hers and, without another word, stepped backward from the curricle. Then, to Colly's surprise, he caught her around the waist with his hands, lifted her from the seat, and swung her to the ground. Without waiting to see if she could stand unaided, he swiftly scooped her up into his arms and carried her into the hotel.

Chapter 8

Trembling from delayed reaction, Colly rested her head upon Ethan's broad and exceedingly comforting chest. Then, unable to stop herself from seeking even more comfort, she slipped her arms around his shoulders and buried her face against the thick column of his neck. Obligingly, her rescuer tightened his arms around her, crushing her against his reassuring warmth. Her senses singing with awareness at the nearness of him, Colly decided she would happily endure an accident a day if at the end of it Ethan would lift her in his arms and hold her tightly against him as he did now.

"Colly," he whispered, the hushed word sounding just above her ear, "I—"

"Colly! Oh, my dear child." Miss Montrose rose from her purloined chair just inside the ladies' reading room and hurried across the foyer toward her niece. "Lord Raymond, whatever has happened?"

"A minor accident only, Miss Montrose. I do not believe your niece received any injury, but perhaps a doctor should be summoned just in case."

"Nonsense," Colly said, finding her voice at last.

"I've sustained no more than a fright, I assure you, and shall be right as a trivet once I have caught my breath."

Lifting her head, Colly wriggled slightly to let Ethan know she could be safely set on her feet, but he blithely ignored the signal, tightening his hold on her waist, then bidding Miss Montrose to precede him up the staircase. Since Colly could do nothing to dissuade him from carrying her all the way to the suite, she gave in as gracefully as possible and returned her face to its newfound home against Ethan's neck.

"I beg of you," Colly said, her face warm with embarrassment at being the center of attention, "let us abandon forever the subject of this afternoon's little mishap." In order to be heard, she was obliged to lift her voice above the chattering of the patrons of the arts seated in the elegant private boxes, as well as the drama lovers milling about on the ground level beneath the boxes, none of whom paid the least attention to the farce being enacted on the stage of the Haymarket Theatre. "If you will, Aunt Pet, I am persuaded that Lady Raymond will find your afternoon's adventures with the royal and near royal vastly amusing."

Thankfully, Miss Montrose was more than happy to comply with her niece's request. Soon she was beguiling the other inhabitants of the box with a recital of the steady stream of visitors who had come to Grillon's that day to pay their respects to Princess Adelaide and to her mother, Duchess Eleanor. As her aunt's discourse progressed, Colly took pains to keep her gaze riveted on the chicken skin fan she held in her hands, the fan whose color exactly matched the mulberry satin of her evening dress—or rather, her mother's evening dress.

Colly dared not look toward the rear of the box, where Ethan sat, lest he read in her eyes what was in her heart. Ever since he had taken his leave of her this afternoon, she had been unable to think of anything for more than two minutes at a time—anything, that is, except the intoxicatingly male scent of his skin, the feel of his powerful arms, and the tingling warmth that seemed to radiate from some unknown source in the center of her being every time she remembered the way he had pressed her body against his.

". . . And I do not hesitate to tell you, Lady Raymond, that in my excitement I very nearly lost my balance while curtsying to His Royal Highness. Quite lowering, I assure you, to be obliged to grab the back of one's chair to keep from falling on one's face at the feet of one's future king." Miss Montrose laughed softly, and her listeners responded in kind, enjoying the older lady's anecdote.

"I declare, I felt like the veriest country bumpkin. But the prince was all graciousness, nodding in my direction before continuing his journey across the foyer to the staircase."

"Prinny's a charmer right enough," Mr. Harrison said. "I wonder, though, ma'am, was he the only one of the royals to visit?"

Colly heard Ethan's soft chuckle and was reminded that Mr. Harrison had some sort of wager on the Duke of Clarence's chances of getting the German princess down the aisle. "Behave, Winny," he cautioned softly.

"Oh, no," Miss Montrose replied pleasantly to Mr. Harrison's question, unaware that the young man's interest was financial rather than romantic. "Shortly after the prince regent's arrival, the duke made his appearance."

Mr. Harrison slapped his knee in glee. "Finally, by Jove. We'll call this *day one*. Ethan, dear boy, I trust you'll serve as my proof. Three's the lucky number."

Her resolve forgotten, Colly turned toward the rear of the box, a smile on her lips for the speaker. With her shoulders already turned in that direction, she decided it would be shabby beyond permission not to vouchsafe a similar smile to the man who sat next to Mr. Harrison.

Not surprisingly, gray-green eyes encountered brown. And held . . . and held.

Millennia later, as if from some distant planet, Colly heard someone speak her name, thankfully breaking the hypnotic spell Ethan had cast over her. "Yes?" she answered, her voice not sounding like her own.

"Miss Sommes," Lady Raymond said, "I was just saying to Miss Montrose that I find all betrothals— royal or otherwise—of immense interest. Do you not find them so?"

For some inexplicable reason Colly felt her face

grow warm at the question. "Betrothals, ma'am? I am sure I have little opinion on the subject."

"Now, now, my dear," Ethan's mother continued, "all young gels dream of their own betrothals. As do they also," she added, her tone almost conspiratorial, "dream of the gentlemen to whom they will someday be betrothed."

"I do assure you, ma'am, I am not among that number."

Growing uncomfortably warm, Colly snapped open the chicken skin fan and began to wave it near her neck, making the tendrils that escaped her chignon dance in the breeze.

Lady Raymond said no more on the subject of betrothals, but her smile possessed some knowing quality that put Colly completely to the blush, making her wave the fan all the faster. But before she could break the delicate ivory sticks, Ethan tapped her on the shoulder and asked her if she would care to stroll about during the intermission.

"Yes, please," she said, standing immediately, "I would love some exercise."

Ethan and Mr. Harrison both stood, though neither of those gentlemen was so bereft of manners as to inform the lady that the intermission had not yet begun. While Mr. Harrison stepped to the rear of the box to open the door, Ethan took Colly's elbow to assist her; then the two of them left the box, blissfully unaware of the smiles exchanged by those who remained.

To Colly's relief, Ethan began almost immediately a discussion of the merits of the farce being presented on stage, keeping that conversation going all the while they strolled along the horseshoe corridor past the doors of the other boxes. Finally, when they reached the end of the corridor and were obliged to turn and retrace their steps, he said, "You must be wondering about my mother's latest catechism."

Colly felt herself blush again. "Not at all, sir. I gave it not the least notice, and have quite forgotten the matter."

To her surprise, Ethan stopped walking and turned to look at her. "Coming it a bit too brown, my girl. The last time I saw you fan yourself with such ferocity, you were enacting me a farce of your own— *The Simpering Miss*—I believe you called the exhibition."

Colly was not immune to the smile that pulled at the corners of Ethan's well-shaped mouth, nor to the teasing light that warmed his eyes. "I?" she said, looking up at him and batting her eyelashes as she had that evening they had played chess at Sommes Grange. "Lah, sir, I believe you have me confused with some other lady, for I have no recollection of the incident."

"A selective memory," he accused, tucking her arm in his and resuming their stroll. "That must simplify life."

"Are you calling me simple?" she asked, all too aware of the muscular arm beneath her hand. "It is too bad in you, sir. First you imply that I prevaricate, next you accuse me of simpering, then you as good as call me a simpleton. What compliment shall I expect next? That I am witless?"

"No, ma'am, acquit me of that, for you have always your wits about you. But I take leave to inform you that you are a jade."

"Now *that* I shall take as a compliment, sir, and thank you prodigiously. Especially if you had in mind that entrancing gem stone so valued in the Orient. Of course, if you have reference to the Spanish *piedra de yjada,* or stone of the side, I must inform you that I am not a cure for a pain in that region of the anatomy."

Ethan threw back his head and laughed. "No, Miss Bluestocking, you are more likely a thorn in the side. And if I were your betrothed, I would be tempted to—"

"I say, Raymond!" bellowed Mr. Philomen Delacourt, effectively silencing Ethan on the extremely interesting subject of what he might be tempted to do if he were Colly's betrothed, and tempting the hypothetical betrothee to wish Ethan's uncle instantly transported to the far reaches of China.

"Fancy meeting you again, Raymond. And you, too, Miss Sommes," he added cordially. "Don't lay my blinkers on you for a twelve-month at a time, nephew, then see you twice in one day. Only consider the odds of that happening."

"Only consider," Ethan repeated dryly.

As though certain of his welcome, Mr. Delacourt fell into step with Ethan and Colly, rattling on for several minutes without getting, or needing, any encouragement from his captive audience. Colly could only guess how long the loquacious gentleman might have continued thus, had he not been stopped mid-monologue by the approach of Lord and Lady Sedgewick, accompanied by a raven-haired young lady whose flawless beauty, thankfully, seemed to take Mr. Delacourt's breath away.

"Good evening," Ethan greeted the newcomers, bowing first over Lady Sedgewick's hand, then over the hand of the lovely young lady. "Lady Sedgewick, my lord, I believe you met Miss Sommes the other evening at your very delightful musicale, but I remember distinctly that your ward was not in attendance that evening. Miss Pilkington, allow me to make you known to Miss Sommes."

Colly exchanged greetings with Lord and Lady Sedgewick, then smiled at the raven-haired beauty who, after the briefest of nods in Colly's direction, returned all her attention to Ethan. "Lord Raymond," she cooed prettily, "how very pleasing, to be sure, knowing that one's absence is noted. May I hope that on the occasion of the ball Auntie Aurelia gives for me in September, you will not be absent?"

Ethan voiced some platitude about time being the master and not the servant of man, but the young lady seemed to perceive that as an affirmative reply. "How delightful, my lord. I shall be certain to save a waltz for you."

Though Ethan did no more than smile in answer to the beauty's invitation, Colly felt an overwhelming desire to box a set of ears. As to whose ears wanted boxing, on that subject she still had not made up her mind when Ethan bade the young lady farewell, explaining that the intermission was nearly over and they must return to their party.

As they walked back to Lady Raymond's box, Mr. Delacourt once again monopolized the conversation, interrupting himself for mere seconds to call greetings to various of his acquaintances. But this time Colly was glad of the gentleman's chatter. She could not have spoken a word if her life depended upon it, for she was busy wrestling with a very new and a very disturbing feeling. Could this be jealousy? If so, she wanted no part of it, for it was, she discovered, a very energy-draining emotion.

Mr. Harrison rose at their entrance and exchanged pleasantries with Ethan's uncle.

"You here, Philomen?" Lady Raymond asked. "I didn't expect to see you this evening."

"Don't mean to stay, Phoebe. Didn't even mean to stop in, actually. Must be still all about in my head from having encountered the Pilkington chit. Beautiful gel. A possible incomparable, I believe. Too bad she had to delay her come-out because of the mourning period, for she'll have her work cut out for her this season, what with the Sommes chit making her bow." He then turned to Colly with a conspiratorial wink. "Be interesting to see how the Pilkington reacts to meeting your sister, Miss Sommes." His laughter at his own joke lasted for several seconds. "By the by," he said, "don't believe you told me the chit's name."

Colly, who had just taken her place at the front of the box, pretended an interest in the occupants of the box directly across from theirs. The ruse did not serve, however, for Miss Montrose filled the breach of her niece's rudeness. "My younger niece is named for the Gillyflower, sir. But we have always called her Gilly."

Even above the cacophony of people reclaiming their seats for the conclusion of the farce, Colly heard Ethan gasp.

"Gilly?" Mr. Harrison said. "By Jove, Ethan, wasn't that the name Reggie wrote in his lett— Demme," he muttered, his back turned to the ladies, "you didn't have to break my toes, dear boy."

Colly had no idea what happened during the final act of the farce; she knew only that the dratted thing seemed to go on forever. All she could think of was that now Ethan knew she was not the girl to whom his brother had become betrothed. Lamenting the fact that she had not told him the truth herself, she felt certain that now he would despise her as a liar, if only a liar by omission.

The curtain finally came down, and the coach ride back to Grillon's was completed. But in that time, thanks to a mental rehashing of all the mistakes she had made in her dealings with Ethan, Colly had managed to worry herself into a blinding headache. She wanted nothing more than to lay her head down on her pillow and give vent to the tears that begged to be shed, but escape was not possible until after she and Miss Montrose had said all that was proper to their hostess.

The amenities completed, Colly allowed Ethan to hand her out of the carriage, but she could not make herself look into his face. Lord Raymond, it appeared, was having none of her reticence, and on the pretext of kissing her hand, he informed her that he would call upon her the next day.

"And," he said, his voice edged with anger, "I expect you to receive me. You owe me that much."

Ten minutes later, after she and Miss Montrose had lit their bedroom candles and proceeded to their separate chambers, Colly discovered that she was to be denied the comfort of her pillow. Her hand had only just touched the doorknob to her room when she heard a scream. A second scream followed almost immediately, but by that time Colly had run across the small sitting room and thrown open the door to her aunt's bedchamber. The chamber was in darkness.

"Aunt Pet, what is it?"

"Colly?" said a frightened voice, "is that you?"

"Mama?"

Her heart still pounding from the fright given her by the screams, Colly stepped inside the room, her candle held high. What she found were two startled ladies, one on either side of the bed. One lady was clad only in her nightdress, clutching a pillow close against her body, as though duck feathers would shield her from evildoers who broke into one's bedchamber in the dark of night. The other lady, fully clothed, held a candle whose flame had died.

Aunt Pet found her voice first. "Violet Sommes, you frightened me out of a year's growth."

"I frightened *you?*" replied Colly's indignant

mother. "It was not I who entered your room in the dark of night and threw back the covers. I imagined myself as near to murdered as made no difference."

"The candle flame blew out," Miss Montrose said by way of apology. "And I had no idea you would be here."

"This is my room," declared Lady Sommes. "Where else would I be?"

"A good question," Colly interposed. "Where have you been, Mama?"

"Gilly and I were invited to—" The lady stopped mid-sentence and gasped. "Colly! Your dress! It is almost a duplicate to a mulberry silk I had made up." Suddenly suspicious, Lady Sommes stepped toward the foot of the bed to get a better look. "That *is* my new dress. Never tell me that you have already worn it about town. How could you be so thoughtless? It is too bad in you, for I had the silk made up especially for a theater party I planned to give during the seas—"

"Never mind about that now, Violet," Miss Montrose said. "I know your sensibilities have been overset, and for that I beg your pardon, but please, let us save all other talk for the morrow. If you feel so inclined after a night's sleep, you may berate us to your heart's content over breakfast."

With a most unladylike *humph*, Lady Sommes crawled back up onto the bed and pulled the covers to her neck.

"Mama," Colly said, "is Gilly with you?"

"Of course not, don't be a ninnyhammer. I was

alone until Aunt Pet entered the room, startling me so that I shall probably never sleep again."

"I meant is Gilly here, at the hotel?"

"Your sister is in her bed. Though how she could sleep through all this racket is more than I can say."

"Colly," Miss Montrose said with a tone that brooked no argument, "I daresay your mama is as exhausted as I am myself, so give me a light from your taper, then run along to your own bed. And try, if you can, not to frighten Gilly out of her wits; I think we've all had quite enough excitement for one night."

"Yes, Aunt."

Obediently lighting her aunt's candle from her own, Colly kissed the wrinkled cheek, then walked around to the other side of the bed and saluted her mother's still youthful one. "The dress is undamaged, Mama."

"I hope it may be so, for I especially—"

"Good night," Miss Montrose said, all but pushing her niece from the room.

Colly was more than happy to quit her mother's room, but she had no intention of going to bed at the present time, not before she'd had a serious talk with a certain flibbertigibbit young lady. With that goal in mind, she hurried across the sitting room and entered the bedroom.

The neat chamber Colly had left only hours ago now gave evidence of her sister's occupancy. A pretty pink traveling dress lay forgotten on the floor, bandboxes spilled their contents onto the nightstand and the dressing table, and the drawers of the mahogany

chiffonier stood open with shifts and wrappers carelessly hanging half in and half out.

Allowing herself only a moment to wonder what
had possessed Norah, Gilly's abigail, to leave such a
clutter until morning, Colly set the candle on the
washstand, then approached the slender lump beneath the messy bed covers. She brushed aside an
open box of bonbons, a novel by Mrs. Edgeworth,
and a wrapper that appeared to have only just come
from the modiste's shop, then sat down on the edge
of the bed. "Gilly," she said, gently tapping the lump.

When she received no response, Colly tapped with
more determination. "Gilly. Wake up, do, for we
need to talk."

"Mrphmmm," her sister mumbled, then turned to
face the far wall.

In a less than charitable mood Colly threw the
covers back, then gave her sister's shoulder a good
shake. "Gilly Sommes, you wake up this instant. I
have every intention of speaking with you before this
night is finished. Since I must also sleep in that bed,
I am loath to throw water on you, but I promise I
will do so if that is what is needed."

Gilly opened one eyelid. "That you, Colly? What is
amiss?"

"You might well ask," her sister replied. "Now
wake up, for I wish you to tell me what you did with
the ring."

The lovely Gilly pushed a thick cloud of wavy
blond hair from her face and opened her eyes. They
were blue eyes, and they had been likened, by more
than one besotted admirer, to sparkling sapphires.

Even now, when their owner had just been roused from sleep, the sapphires had not lost their luster. "What did I do with what ring? Colly, if you have lost some silly ring, I swear it was none of my doing. Must I remind you that I am no longer a child who rummages through her big sister's things? Furthermore, I take it amiss that you would awaken me just because you lost some bauble that might just as easily be searched for in the mor—"

"The betrothal ring!" Colly almost shouted, giving her sister another shake. "And do not try to fob me off by pretending you do not understand me, you foolish girl, for I know you entered into a clandestine betrothal."

Gilly sat up quickly, her eyes wide with surprise. "Betrothal? I nev—" Even as the denial formed on her lips, the chit's eyes registered comprehension. "Oh, that. Pshaw, Colly, that was nothing. But how did you find out?"

"Depend upon it," Colly said through clenched teeth, "secrets, especially those concerning clandestine betrothals, have a way of getting out. Now, before I lose all patience, where is the Bradford Diamond?"

Chapter 9

"But I never dreamed the diamond was real," Gilly wailed. "Honest, Colly. For it is the size of a walnut and quite dreadfully gaudy. I thought it was some gimcrack he had purchased at a fair. Besides," the chit added, lifting her chin dramatically, "you must know I would never have taken a real ring, especially not from some young man I had met only two days before."

If the young lady meant this artless declaration to denote some degree of common sense, she misjudged her audience.

"Have your wits gone lacking, Gilly? Had you no thought whatsoever to your reputation if this should get out?"

Gilly lifted her beautiful shoulders. "But how could it get out? It was but a lark. I do not even remember the young man's name. He was just some friend of Ione Kittridge's brother. You remember Ione Kittridge. She and I were at Miss Tilson's School together."

"The young man's name is Bradford," Colly pronounced soberly. "Reggie Bradford."

Her sister nodded her head, causing her flaxen tresses to sway in the candlelight. "That sounds familiar. If you say that is his name, I believe you. I really did not attend to most of what he said. He talked such foolishness—schoolboy foolishness about the larks he and Mr. Kittridge have been up to since they were sent down from Eton. Boxing the watch, that sort of thing. I found it all quite boring."

Colly felt a strong urge to give her beautiful sister another shake. "If you found him so boring, why did you accept the ring? Why did you allow him to propose in the first place?"

"Practice," she replied artlessly.

"What!"

Gilly tucked her legs beneath her and arranged the cover more comfortably. "Colly, I want to make the most of my come-out. I plan to attend every party, dance every single dance, and flirt with all the gentlemen. I mean to enjoy every minute of the season, for I shall probably be betrothed by the time I return to Sommes Grange."

Disturbed by this statement, Colly took her sister's hand in hers. "You need not do so," she advised softly, "not if your heart is not engaged."

Gilly laughed. "Of course my heart will be engaged, pea goose. With all the handsomest men to choose from, how could I not form a *tendre* for one of them? And when the man I love comes to beg for my hand, I will know how to behave, because I

practiced the entire scene already on Mr. Brim-
ford."

"Bradford," Colly corrected with a sigh of resignation. One might as well try to teach cattle to fly as to
seek to convince her romantic sister that her season
might not go exactly as she had planned. "I think we
should save this particular conversation for another
day. Preferably a day when I am not plagued with a
headache and in need of sleep."

Colly slid off the bed and began searching
through the chaos for her nightdress. "I have it in
mind to rise quite early on the morrow so that I may
return the betrothal ring to Lord Raymond before
he is up and about. Since I am persuaded you do
not wish to rise that early, I suggest you get the ring
for me now, so I will not need to wake you in the
morning. You cannot know how much trouble this
has caused, nor how much I wish to be rid of the
thing."

"But, Colly," Gilly said, her hands spread palms
up, as if to show they concealed nothing. "I cannot
give you the ring."

Colly could almost hear warning bells toll inside
her head. Her lips barely moved. "Why can you not?"

"For the simple reason that I no longer have it. I
gave it away."

"You gave it—" Colly forced her voice to remain
calm. "To whom?"

"To Norah. I was afraid Mama might find the ring
and give me a scold, so when Norah admired it, I
said she could have it."

Feeling somewhat like Damocles with the sword

hanging over his head, Colly remembered the question she had asked herself when she first came into the room and saw the clothes strewn about. "Why has Norah not picked up this room?"

"Oh, she's not here," Gilly replied airily.

Her patience at an end, Colly threatened to draw and quarter her sister if she did not tell her the whole story immediately.

At the sight of Colly's rigid face, tears began to spill from Gilly's eyes. "Mama and I were fagged out from all the shopping and the interminable trips to the dressmakers for fittings, so when Mrs. Kittridge—Ione's grandmother—asked if we would like to drive down with them to her son's home to rest and to breathe some fresh country air, Mama agreed we might. It is a very pretty place, Colly, situated but a short drive from town, and it quite put me in mind of the Grange. I am persuaded you would like it prodigiously if—"

"Cut line, Gilly. Where is Norah?"

"We left her at Aymesley. The reason Ione's mother did not come to town to help her choose her come-out clothes is because the three younger children all are down with the chicken pox. The children were most fractious, and you know how good Norah is in the sick room—always knowing just when a pillow wants fluffing or when a person needs a cool drink. So when Mrs. Kittridge—Ione's mother, that is—begged Mama, practically on bended knee, to let Norah stay, she could not refuse.

"Not to worry, though," Gilly added naively, "the

hotel has maids, so I am persuaded we shan't miss Norah overmuch."

"I miss her already," Colly muttered, glancing around the messy room. Then she asked, "How far is it to Aymesley?"

"Less than two hours. I cannot be more exact, because Mrs. Kittridge was forever making the driver stop the coach, then obliging us to alight in order to view some horrid old bridge or a pile of tumbled-down stones she insisted were of historical significance. As though we cared for such fustian. I tell you, Colly, I never expected such shabby treatment."

Colly ignored her sister's grimace of distaste. "Less than two hours. You are sure?"

"Well, not cocksure, because I slept most of the way back. But it is quite close. Because of its nearness, Ione has invited Mama and me to repair there at any time if we should begin to grow fagged during the hectic season." The significance of her sister's question suddenly penetrated Gilly's self-absorbed mind. "Why do you ask?"

"Because," Colly replied, her thoughts on the interview Ethan had threatened, "I mean to have that ring in my possession before Eth—that is, before the day is out."

As it transpired, Colly's good intentions were thwarted by nature. The skies opened up early the next day and dumped enough rain on London to render the out-of-doors fit only for sailors and ducks. Since Colly was neither, she was obliged to postpone her trip to Aymesley. She prayed that Ethan would be similarly deterred in his plans to visit her, but in that instance she misjudged her man.

One might even say she misjudged her men, for the next day their sitting room overflowed with morning callers. Only Lady Sommes was absent, claiming the headache as a result of the thoughtless assault upon her nerves the previous evening.

The first rain-soaked visitor to arrive was Gilly's bosom bow, Miss Ione Kittridge, a rather plain-faced damsel possessed of scarcely half Gilly's physical charms and even less of her intellect. Arrayed in a walking dress of palest yellow lutestring, three-quarters of which was covered by a biscuit-colored pelisse, Miss Kittridge showed to a decided disadvantage when seated beside Gilly, who was dressed simply in a celestial blue morning dress of Spitalfields silk that set off her creamy skin and blue eyes to perfection.

However, the most unfortunate circumstance, at least by Colly's reckoning, was the young lady's tendency to make Gilly appear a veritable scholar by comparison. When Colly asked the chit for directions to her home, explaining that an item of quite expensive jewelry had been inadvertently left in Norah's possession, Miss Kittridge could give but a sketchy reply.

"For Tom Coachman always drives, don't you know? But if you should wish to travel there, Tom Coachman is returning home as soon as the weather permits; he could drive you down."

"A wonderful suggestion," Gilly said, smiling at her friend and then at her sister. "At school I could always depend upon Ione to help me figure out the best way to go about a thing."

One had only to picture such a situation to wonder that either young lady had survived to enjoy their coming season, especially since neither of the needle wits seemed to grasp the fact that the coachman's trip home would be one way. In no frame of mind to waste instruction upon lightweights, Colly was provoked into retorting, "How fortunate Gilly is to be numbered among your friends, Miss Kittridge, for I do not scruple to surmise that you were called upon many times to help extricate her from the consequences of her own folly."

Observing the puzzled expression in the damsel's eyes, Colly felt her own face grow warm, knowing herself mean-spirited for having dueled with an unarmed opponent. Miss Kittridge had no part in Colly's troubles, and it was unfair to take her megrims out on the innocent young lady. Just as it was useless to vent her frustrations upon her not-so-innocent sister, for it would appear that Gilly had forgotten it was she who had precipitated the entire debacle of the ring. Alas, one might as well whistle in the wind.

With nothing to be gained by lingering in the company of the young ladies, Colly declined Miss Kittridge's offer to ride with their coachman. She excused herself on the pretext of needing to write a letter. The pretext abandoned once she reached the bedchamber, she spent the time alone staring at the walls and wondering how she could get to

Aymesley before Ethan confronted her regarding her deceit.

When Colly returned to the sitting room some time later, she was surprised to discover not only her sister, her Aunt Pet, and Miss Kittridge, but also Mr. Harrison and Lord Raymond. The two young ladies perched prettily on the edge of the small rose damask sofa, where they listened raptly, but contributed nothing, to the conversation being borne completely by Miss Montrose and Mr. Harrison, who sat in the two side chairs opposite the sofa.

Colly did not immediately espy Ethan, for he stood across the room, gazing out the rain-soaked window at the view of Albemarle Street. Only when Mr. Harrison bade her hallo did Ethan turn from the window, catching Colly's attention and putting her at pains to conceal her quickly drawn breath.

Ethan noted the stifled gasp, however, and gave her a sardonic smile that told her he had been waiting, and not very patiently, for her arrival. She felt a shiver of apprehension steal down her spine, but unwilling to let Ethan think she had been hiding out, afraid to face him, she lifted her chin and returned his smile, bestowing upon him a look she hoped was friendly yet devoid of the least sign of toadying. Had she but known the effect of that smile upon the mocking gentleman, she would have felt immeasurably better.

For his part, Ethan felt as though he had just been dealt a flush hit to the solar plexus. The beautiful smile, so unexpected, very nearly robbed his mind of his reason for calling upon Colly on such a miserable day. Not that it mattered if he forgot his purpose, for the limited space in the sitting room, plus the number of people present, made private conversation impossible.

"Well met, Miss Sommes," Mr. Harrison greeted, offering her his chair and drawing up a tapestried Carolean chair for himself. "I was just describing to Miss Montrose and the young ladies the various displays they might expect to see at Vauxhall Gardens should they venture there."

Happy to pursue any subject other than the one for which Ethan had come, Colly joined the ladies and Mr. Harrison and added a recollection of her own about a cascade—she thought it had been called the Alpine Adventure—that had been quite popular when she was last in town.

Lord Raymond still had not spoken a word since Colly's arrival, but he was watching her. Oh, how he was watching her. Colly could feel his intense gaze from across the room; it was sending nervous ripples down her neck. Of its own accord her hand lifted to touch her nape, but once she realized what she was about, she covered the movement by pretending to adjust an errant hairpin.

Ethan watched Colly lift her hand to the loose chignon at the nape of her neck. From the moment she had entered the sitting room, he had been thinking her unaffected by his presence. But as she sought to secure a hairpin that had worked itself free, he saw the slight trembling of her fingers and knew she was not nearly as unmoved as her serene countenance would have him believe. The knowledge pleased him immeasurably and went a long way toward calming his own emotions.

Not that he blamed Colly overmuch for letting him believe it was her to whom his brother had become betrothed. Two minutes in the same room with her young sister was enough to convince him that protecting the reputation of that hey-go-mad miss was, more than likely, a full-time occupation. Unless he missed his guess, the chit had probably been the object of lovesick swains since she was in short skirts, for she was as pretty as she could stare.

He agreed with his uncle Philomen's prediction that Miss Gilly would give Miss Pilkington a run for the money in the race for the honors as the season's incomparable. Her fair tresses were a perfect foil for the Pilkington chit's raven locks.

Of course, his uncle was all about in his head to suggest that Gilly outshone her sister! To compare Gilly's blue-eyed, girlish prettiness to Colly's exquisite beauty was ludicrous. Looking at them side by side, Ethan could only wonder at his uncle's lack of discernment.

Yes, Ethan could understand Colly's wanting to protect her much younger sister. After all, it was no more than he had done for Reggie. Admitting that fact went a long way toward calming his anger at Colly for having misled him.

And if he was to admit the real truth, the thing that rankled most was the torment Colly had put him through by allowing him to believe that her affections were otherwise engaged. That little piece of playacting had cost Ethan dearly. He had been dragged through hell and back picturing Colly pining away for his brother, and he thought it only fair that she get a little of her own back.

With retaliation in mind, Lord Raymond strolled over to the two young ladies. His object: a little flirtation. He hoped to awaken in Colly some of the feelings of jealousy he had been wrestling with for the better part of a week. "Miss Gilly," he began, "I believe you are acquainted with my brother, Reggie."

Colly gasped. She had not expected this; Ethan was not the kind of man to spar with an unequal opponent. As soon as the thought formed itself in her mind, however, she knew that it was the absolute truth, and the knowledge let her relax. Whatever maggot Ethan had got in his head, his scheme was not to punish Gilly but to punish her.

"Your brother?" Gilly asked, not deceiving anyone with her wide-eyed stare. "I, uh. That is—"

"Reggie Bradford," Miss Kittridge supplied obligingly. "You remember him, Gill. He is a particular friend of my brother's. They are at school together."

Ethan looked closely at the young lady, who had spoken scarcely two words since he and Winny entered the sitting room. She must be the sister of that addlepate Reggie was always dragging around. Yes, now that he looked, he could detect a superficial resemblance, though Miss Kittridge had, fortunately, escaped the jug-handle ears so difficult to ignore on her sibling. And judging from the fact that the girl had just managed to put two sentences together while her brother seemed to communicate solely by grunts and words of one syllable, Ethan deemed the chit to be not only the best-looking of the Kittridges but also the repository for the family brains.

"I believe the more accurate statement, Miss Kittridge, is that Reggie and your brother are 'sent down' from school together."

To that sally the young lady returned a blank stare, leading Ethan to assume that her conversational skills had reached their limit. Whereupon, he turned his attention back to her friend. "Word of your beauty has preceded you, Miss Gilly. And you cannot know how very refreshing it is to discover that some things one is told are true."

At this last, Ethan looked pointedly at Colly. Unfortunately, his intended prey was otherwise occupied, busy adjusting one of the half dozen ribbons of her Marie sleeved morning dress.

Gilly, however, hearing only the compliment, and finding this a very pleasing topic of conversation, gave Lord Raymond her full attention. Smiling her prettiest, she said, "You are very kind, my lord."

"And you are very kind, Miss Gilly, to smile at me in that most enchanting manner."

Ethan's voice held a deep, admiring note that made Gilly's eyes sparkle and made Colly's temper sizzle. *How dare he flirt with Gilly? And why did not Aunt Pet call the silly chit to heel for making such a spectacle of herself?*

"I had already heard it rumored that you were a

diamond of the first water," Ethan continued, "but now that we have met, I must say the rumor is inaccurate."

"Sir?" Gilly replied coyly, all too aware that another compliment was in the offing.

Ethan lifted her hand almost to his lips and looked teasingly into her blue eyes. "Not a diamond, Miss Gilly, but a sapphire. And most definitely of the first water."

Gilly batted her eyelashes, not at all averse to such teasing from one who was obviously a man about town. "Lah, sir."

Although memories of other, more fascinating eyelashes came to Ethan's mind, he pushed the recollection aside and smiled as though he found the child's attempt at flirtation captivating. "I predict that once the young bucks cast their eyes upon you, you will be obliged to remove the knocker from your door to keep the gentlemen from—"

Whatever outrageous prediction he had meant to voice, he was forced to keep it to himself, for their conversation was interrupted by a scratch at the door. A fact for which at least one of the Sommes ladies was most grateful. *At least he had not tipped the entire butter boat upon her sister!*

Thinking the maid must have arrived with a tea tray, Colly hurried to the door. At this point any diversion was welcome. However, it was not the maid but one of the hotel footmen who stood in the hallway. The man touched his finger to his forehead respectfully, then proffered a silver salver bearing a gentleman's calling card.

"The gentleman is waiting in the foyer, miss, and wants to know if the ladies are receiving."

Colly read the card, then instinctively looked at Ethan. "I, uh . . ."

Perceiving her confusion, Ethan stepped forward and took the thin white pasteboard from her unresisting fingers, reading the name engraved upon the card. "It is George FitzClarence," he said softly, for her ears only. "Do you know him?"

Colly shook her head. "No. I mean, of course I know who he is, but we have never been introduced. I am at a loss as to what is best to do."

"Do you wish to be guided by me?"

"Yes, please."

Ethan set the card back on the salver, along with a sovereign. "Please ask Mr. FitzClarence to join us."

"Yes, m'lord," the man said, his eyes alight at the gold coin.

The moment the door was shut, Colly turned to her aunt. "Aunt Pet, we are to have a visitor. Mr. George FitzClarence."

The older lady's hand went to her mouth in surprise. "The Duke of Clarence's son?"

"The Duke of Clarence has a son?" Miss Kittridge asked, once again ill-choosing her moment to enter the conversation. "But I thought he was marrying soon in hopes of producing an heir."

"An *heir*, you goose," her bosom bow elucidated. "His son is a *Fitz*. Surely you know—"

"Enough!" instructed Miss Montrose. "I want not one more word from either of you. If you wish to be treated as adults, you must show some semblance of having attained the status." The young misses properly subdued, Miss Montrose returned her attention to Colly. "My dear, how came you to meet him?"

"I did not, Aunt."

Unobtrusively Ethan touched Colly's elbow and led her back to the chair she had vacated. "Winny and I have known George for years, Miss Montrose. Depend upon it, you will find him a charming and unexceptional gentleman."

"By Jove, yes," Mr. Harrison agreed, "known him for donkey's years. You will meet him everywhere. Always received, don't you know?"

When the knock came, Ethan opened the door. "FitzClarence," he greeted affably, his hand extended in welcome, "do come in. Allow me to make you known to the ladies."

The young man shook Lord Raymond's hand. "I did not expect to find you here, Raymond, but 'tis a pleasant surprise, I assure you."

"George," Mr. Harrison greeted, "should have known you would discover where the prettiest ladies might be found."

"Winny. You here, too?"

Mr. George FitzClarence, eldest of the Duke of Clarence's ten children with the actress Dorothy Jordan, was a young man of about Colly's age. Though bearing a strong resemblance to the Hanovers, his looks were aided considerably by the inheritance of a goodly portion of his mother's reputed beauty, and to that attraction was added the further appeal of a very smart military uniform. While Miss Montrose and Colly were in silent agreement that he was a tolerably handsome man, the two younger ladies, had their opinions been sought, would have happily declared Mr. George FitzClarence "slap up to the echo!"

Ethan introduced the new arrival to the ladies, then watched as he bowed over each hand, showing a finesse that was more reminiscent of his uncle the prince regent than of his rough-around-the-edges father, the Duke of Clarence. Ethan relaxed at this show of pretty manners, for Mr. FitzClarence, though illegitimate, considered himself royal and had been known on more than one occasion to behave with what Ethan considered an unbecoming arrogance.

"I have come," the visitor said once the amenities were completed, "as an emissary of my future stepmother, the princess Adelaide of Saxe-Meiningen."

This piece of news was received by all with wide-eyed surprise. Only Miss Montrose found her voice, and that was barely above a whisper. "The princess," she said.

"Yes, ma'am. The princess Adelaide is aware that someone, I believe it must have been you, ma'am," he said, bowing slightly to Colly, "was of assistance to one of her ladies-in-waiting. At Canterbury, I believe it was. The princess has asked me to express to you her appreciation for your kindness."

Colly felt her face grow warm with pleasure. "I was most happy to be of assistance, Mr. Fitz-

Clarence. Though, in truth, it was a mere politeness, the kind of thing one would do for any stranger. Let me assure you, sir, it is *I* who am beholden to Her Highness. For her graciousness."

Mr. FitzClarence concurred affably. "The princess is indeed a most gracious lady. As our future step-mama, she was quite interested to hear a few stories of my sisters and brothers, as well as of her new home at Bushy."

None of his listeners vouchsafed a reply to Mr. FitzClarence's observations. They were all too stunned by the information that the lady who might one day be the queen of England had been intro-duced to her husband's by-blows. Not to mention the even further staggering revelation that the princess was expected to undertake the role of "step-mama" to the duke's five sons and five daughters.

To Colly's relief, the maid arrived at just that mo-ment with the tea tray, and no more was said about what was, to her, as uncomfortable a visit as she had ever endured. Happy to be occupied, Colly poured while Ethan passed the cups around. Thus engaged, she was unable to follow all the conversation until everyone was served.

"There is to be a double wedding," Mr. Fitz-Clarence replied in answer to a question put to him by Miss Montrose. " 'Twill be held in the queen's drawing room at Kew. My uncle the Duke of Kent and his new duchess, Victoria, will say their vows alongside my father and the princess Adelaide. Both the brides will be given in marriage by my uncle the prince regent."

When Mr. FitzClarence had concluded his story of the coming royal nuptials, Miss Montrose was obliged to resort to her handkerchief, for tears of joy streamed down her cheeks. "Is it not the most romantic of stories?"

The two young ladies concurred, underscoring Miss Montrose's lachrymose remarks with a few dainty sniffs of their own. And though the gentlemen nodded politely, Mr. Harrison could not be expected to enter into their sentiments wholeheartedly, for he had apparently lost his wager.

From the talk of the royal weddings, George Fitz-Clarence progressed to one or two amusing stories of his rough-and-tumble sisters and brothers, and their seemingly idyllic life at Bushy, the Duke of Clarence's home. "I shall be traveling down there tomorrow," he said, "to see how my sisters are getting along."

"Bushy?" said Miss Ione Kittridge, forgetting Miss Montrose's earlier admonition and intruding upon a conversation to which she had been quietly listening for the better part of an hour. "Is not Bushy quite near Aymesley?"

"I believe it is," Mr. FitzClarence replied, not best pleased at having been interrupted, especially by a plain-faced chit just out of the schoolroom.

"Miss Sommes," Miss Kittridge declared happily, "there is your answer."

"My answer?"

"Yes, ma'am," replied the keeper of the Kittridge

brains, "Mr. FitzClarence is going to Bushy tomorrow; he can drive you to Aymesley."

It was a contest as to who was more surprised by this artless arrangement of the lives of two people who had been acquainted for less than an hour, but Colly was certainly the most embarrassed. "Oh, no! What I mean to say—"

"Happy to be of service," the young gentleman declared politely, if rather stiffly.

"No need to trouble yourself, FitzClarence," Ethan said in his usual unruffled drawl, "for Miss Sommes is promised to ride with me tomorrow." Then, in a teasing voice, he added, "I hope, ma'am, that you do not mean to cast me aside in favor of a pretty uniform."

"Of course I do not, Lord Raymond," Colly answered, ready to fling herself at his feet in gratitude for extricating her from a truly embarrassing situation. Then, to keep from giving offense, she bestowed upon Mr. FitzClarence a smile that was warmer, friendlier than was her usual manner with strangers. "Not tomorrow, at any rate."

Ethan drew in his breath at that smile. It started on Colly's lovely lips and quickly ignited a teasing light in her mysterious gray-green eyes. It was a smile he had come to think of as belonging to him alone, and he realized with some heat that he disliked thoroughly having it bestowed on anyone other than himself.

And to Ethan's further annoyance, FitzClarence seemed not to realize he had no right to be receiving Colly's smiles. Smiling at her in return, the duke's son vowed himself more than pleased to drive her any place she wished to go. "And at any time, ma'am."

The moment was got through smoothly enough, but Ethan was left with a disquieting desire to blow a hole through George FitzClarence's pretty uniform.

Not many minutes later, the uniformed gentleman declared himself promised elsewhere and took his leave, bidding everyone present a good day. Following his departure, Mr. Harrison and Ethan began their good-byes. It was at the door that Ethan finally got a private moment with Colly.

"Unless tomorrow's weather prohibits it, I shall call for you around ten."

"Tomorrow?"

"Aymesley," he replied.

"Oh, but, surely you did not mean—"

"Around ten," he reiterated. "You were fortunate today," he said very softly, so that only she could hear. "The rain prohibited me from whisking you out for a drive, and the room was too crowded for the private conversation I had intended."

"I know," Colly said, still in very good humor with him for his adroit handling of the Kittridge chit's faux pas, "and I am most truly sorry. For I know you were wanting an opportunity to box my ears."

Her words were spoken so softly that Ethan was obliged to lean very close to hear them, and standing so near to Colly, he could detect a hint of lemon verbena, the fragrance he had come to think of as hers alone. Unable to stop himself, he let his gaze linger on the soft ivory earlobes that peeped tantalizingly from beneath her loosely draped hair. *Box her ears, indeed.* "Madam," he said, his voice suddenly husky, "you do not have the first clue as to what I want to do to you."

Chapter 10

As soon as all the visitors were gone, Colly sat down and wrote a note to the elder Mrs. Kittridge, asking the lady for directions to her son's home in Aymesley. Restating the story she had told Ione Kittridge about Lady Sommes leaving an expensive piece of jewelry with the maid Norah, Colly sent the note around to the Kittridges' Cavendish Square town house.

Within the hour, the footman returned with a three-page missive from Mrs. Kittridge. After expressing her regret that Miss Sommes must put herself to the trouble of retrieving the jewelry, the lady filled in the remainder of the pages with instructions. Instructions more detailed, Colly felt sure, than those followed by the Crusaders on their quest for the Holy Grail.

If the thoroughness of the letter was any indication of the older lady's style of disseminating information, Colly could well imagine the tedium of her sister's trip in the lady's company. Vowing to apologize to Gilly for her lack of sympathy as regarded those many stops for historical enlightenment, Colly was about to interrupt her sister's avid perusal of the latest edition of *La Belle Assemblee* when she heard someone scratch at the door.

Upon opening the door, Colly discovered a liveried footman, his arms loaded with a large and very beautiful arrangement of flowers. "For the ladies in suite twenty-seven," said the servant, proffering the card, though from the livery, Colly could guess by whom he was employed. The signature consisted of only one name, "Raymond."

"My first flowers in London," Gilly declared, tossing her magazine aside and jumping up to smell the mixture of country flowers. "These are marvelous, to be sure, but I would have preferred roses. I wonder why Lord Raymond did not discover our preferences?"

"I cannot say," Colly replied. Though for her part, she thought roses exceedingly boring. Moreover, she found the mixture of daffodils, daisies, and wild snapdragons, accented as they were with petunias, violets, gillyflowers, and columbines, a much more imaginative and very much more personal choice.

"This offering took planning," Colly said, trying not to read more into it than might have been intended. "While anyone may procure roses."

The young lady heard little of her sister's words. "Once the season begins, I shall have roses by the dozens, for I shall let it be known that they are my favorite. But for now, I shall enjoy these country flowers."

After taking the card from Colly's hand, Gilly studied the signature for a moment, her brow wrinkling in concentration as her thoughts took a new direction. "You know what it is, Colly? I am persuaded that you have refined too much upon the matter of the missing betrothal ring. For depend upon it, Lord Raymond would not be sending us flowers if he were as angry as you seem to believe."

Not wanting to argue the matter, Colly said merely that she was in hopes of having the matter of the ring settled once and for all by this time tomorrow.

"Well I hope you may," Gilly offered magnanimously, "for I should like it of all things to invite Lord Raymond to my ball. He would add considerably to my consequence, do you not think?" Not waiting for a response, the damsel continued, "In addition to his title and wealth, he is a most charming gentleman, and quite handsome into the bargain." Then, with a sigh of regret, "It is such a pity he is a bit on the old side."

"Old! You foolish child. Ethan Bradford is no more than one-and-thirty years of age. He—" Colly caught herself in time, moderating the tone of her voice before Gilly became suspicious of her sister's overheated words and begin to wonder at her championship of Lord Raymond. Fortunately, that damsel never lingered over long on any one topic and had already resumed her perusal of *La Belle Ensemblee*, paying little heed to anything outside its pages.

The next day dawned fresh and clear, as invigorating as the previous day had been dismal, so Colly prepared herself for the trip to Aymesley with Lord

Raymond. True to his word, that "aged" gentleman arrived at exactly ten of the clock. With his coat of corbeau superfine and his biscuit pantaloons fitting his athletic physique almost like a second skin, his cravat beautifully arranged in the mathematical, and his top boots shined to an inch, he was, without question, the handsomest man Colly had ever seen.

Miss Gilly Sommes might consider one-and-thirty an advanced age, but her sister did not concur. Moreover, Colly could not believe there was a gentleman in the entire kingdom more imbued with masculine vitality than Ethan Bradford. Nor was there a gentleman more likely to set a woman's heart fluttering within her breast, exactly as Colly's was fluttering at the moment.

"You are refreshingly prompt," Ethan said, smiling at her in a way that made her breath catch in her throat. "One of your many admirable qualities."

"You will do well to remember those qualities, sir, when all your acquaintances turn to stare at you for escorting a veritable dowd."

Noting the playful glint in her eyes, Ethan let his gaze travel from her dove gray carriage dress, still bearing its mourning trim, to her matching kid gloves and half boots. He found nothing to dislike in the costume except the straw Coburg bonnet, which effectively concealed her beautiful hair from his scrutiny.

He gave her a quizzing look.

"Perhaps you recall the carriage dress I wore the other day when we drove in the park?"

"The peach cambric?"

"Yes. It was my mother's—only just arrived from the modiste's. I am afraid it suffered worse than I did when Mr. Harrison's horses shied. Unfortunately, my mother discovered the rent in the hem before I could have it repaired."

Ethan chuckled. "Rang a peal over you, did she?"

"Didn't she just! I am forbidden to so much as glance toward her chamber, never mind laying a single finger upon the doorknob. And as for even *thinking* of borrowing anything of hers ever again, well, sir . . . Actually, I believe I will spare your blushes by not relating to you the remainder of my mother's strictures, for they show an embarrassing want of parental tolerance—nay, devotion. And had I not been present, I would never have credited her quite scathing animadversions regarding persons who are so lacking in character as to borrow an evening dress she had put aside for a most particular occasion."

Her listener nodded sagely. "I collect Lady Sommes caught you in the mulberry satin."

Colly merely rolled her eyes heavenward, eliciting another chuckle from Ethan. "So, since my mother could not see her way clear to allowing me to mutilate another of her new dresses, I am obliged to be seen abroad in last year's frock. And you, sir, since you were so kind as to offer to take me to Aymesley, are obliged to be seen in the company of a dowd. If you wish to cry craven, now is your chance."

"I believe my credit with the *ton* will withstand the association."

"I hope you may be right, my lord."

"And I hope you will soon end this foolishness, ma'am, for you are, as always, a pleasure to behold."

They had arrived at the grand stairway, and Ethan offered her his arm. A good thing, since Colly's knees showed a tendency toward weakness at his very unexpected compliment.

Nothing more was said until Colly was escorted to a striking new Tilbury, its sides and upholstery finished in a very dark green and its trim highlighted in muted yellow. "Now this, sir, is a pleasure to behold. And though I profess to know little of light carriages, I venture to say this is *not* last year's model."

Acknowledging her quip with a smile, Ethan handed Colly up onto the leather-covered box seat. "It is the latest thing, but I believe you will find it performs quite well on the roads. Depend upon it, you need have no concern for your safety."

"With you at the reins," she said, "I will not be concerned."

Ethan took his place beside her. Then, because the drive would exceed the confines of town, and a chaperon of sorts was required, he called, "Up you go, lad," to the tiger who stood at the heads of the spirited black-maned bays.

"Yes, m'lord," the youngster called happily. Then he scurried around to the rear of the two-wheeled Tilbury and leapt up to the platform.

The traffic on the busy streets was as perilous as ever, teeming with pedestrians, laborers, tinkers, packmen, peddlers' carts, and drays of every description; all of which mingled, sometimes disastrously, with Corinthians on horseback, ladies being driven in their carriages, and gentlemen tooling about in their sporting vehicles. The cacophony, too, was a mixture: shouts, screams, curses, and animal noises. Not wanting to add to either situation, Colly sat quietly, with her hands folded in her lap.

After they had crossed the Thames and were winding their way through green trees and pastureland, Ethan let the horses have their heads for a time until some of their freshness was exercised away. Colly found the speed exhilarating, but she was quite happy when they reached the little village of Wimbledon, where Ethan curbed the animals to let them catch their breath.

While the tiger led the bays to the edge of a shallow stream where they could sip from the gently flowing water, Colly and Ethan went for a short stroll, stopping at the charming old stone bridge that crossed the stream. With water in good supply, the banks of the stream were practically overrun with blue forget-me-nots, yellow flag, and the ubiquitous dandelion.

"I wonder," Colly said as they paused to gaze at the lowly flowers, "if this bridge has any historical significance."

"I shouldn't think so. It cannot be more than a century old. Were you desirous of seeing points of historical interest, Miss Bluestocking?"

"I? Acquit me, sir. I was merely remembering Gilly's story of her own trip through this neighborhood."

After Colly explained to him about the elder Mrs.

Kittridge's edifying lectures on the local antiquities, she and Ethan enjoyed a laugh at the young ladies' expense.

"I cannot think how it is," Ethan remarked, still smiling, "that a country capable of producing some of the world's greatest minds sees fit to produce generation after generation of beautiful ninnyhammers."

"The answer is simple," Colly retorted, defending her sex, "those great minds to which you refer are sadly outnumbered by legions of fools and slow-tops. And should anything of substance be taught the young ladies, they might discover for themselves just how vacuous are the minds of the gentlemen they must marry. Imagine the upheaval to society if the ladies refused to surrender control of their lives and their fortunes to the aforementioned fools. Then where, I ask you, would civilization be?"

"A proper poser," Ethan replied. "Let me see if I have the gist of your theory, for I make no pretensions to being one of the great minds. Though," he added, "I trust I do not number among the slowest of the slow-tops. You hypothesize, ma'am, that for the continuation of civilization, it is necessary for females to improve their beauty rather than their brains because the male of the species ogles more efficiently than he thinks."

"I knew I could trust to your perspicacity, sir."

"Accolades from a bluestocking. I thank you, ma'am."

Judging this foolishness to have continued long enough, Colly asked Ethan about a subject that had been on her mind since their meeting with his uncle.

"Mr. Philomen Delacourt mentioned something of your interest in schools. I would like to hear your views on the subject, for I am even now involved in our local Sunday school, trying to reduce the cost—which is, by our standards, nominal—so that even the poorest children may attend. For how are they — the girls as well as the boys—ever to improve their lot if they are denied the rudiments of reading, writing, and simple mathematics?"

"Quite true."

Ethan had been watching her as she spoke, and it seemed to Colly that he found her views of interest. "I believe your uncle said you mean to take your seat in Parliament."

"Yes, but only if I feel I can be of service in that capacity. A year or so back, a parliamentary committee was formed to look into the possibility of educating London's poor. I would like access to the data the committee has compiled on the various schools across the nation. We must begin to build upon what is good in the present systems—and there is much that is good. Unfortunately, there is also much that needs immediate attention."

"I hope you mean to start with the poor quality of the instruction."

"That is my second objective," he answered. "First and foremost, immediate attention must be given to the buildings themselves. I do not believe that children should be forced to spend days and years in environments that breed disease. Unventilated classrooms, unsanitary buildings, often times even damp and musty basements, are deemed acceptable places for the instruction of the young. Conditions such as these must not be tolerated, for in the final analysis, ignoring the plight of the children will affect us all. I fear we do indeed reap what we sow."

They spoke at length on the subject and found themselves in accord on most issues. On those points about which they held differing views, each listened carefully to the other's thoughts, often introducing facts not previously known by the other. Continuing in this vein, they returned to the Tilbury and resumed the drive to Aymesley.

It was a picturesque route, and Colly soon found herself caught up in the simple joy of being in the country. Unashamedly, she filled her lungs with the fresh, clean air, then exhaled noisily, letting the act cleanse her of the taint of London's soot.

"Glad you came?"

"Umm," she answered. And she was glad. The day was lovely, and since she knew she would soon have the Bradford Diamond in her hand and could return it to Ethan, that knowledge rendered her free to enjoy his company.

"Not sorry you came with me," he asked, "when you might have had George FitzClarence?"

"As to that, sir, whatever answer I give, it will be a serious breach of good manners. If I voice a desire to have ridden in Mr. FitzClarence's company, I shall most certainly appear ungrateful to you when you have been so kind as to drive me here. However, if I profess a preference for your company over his, it might well set you up in your own conceit." She sighed. "How is a one to know how to go on?"

"How indeed, viper. You certainly would not wish to pander to my vanity. No point in sparing my feelings, however, for I know it is moon madness with you ladies once you have seen a fellow decked out in his pretty uniform."

"True, my lord, there is something particularly dashing about a gentleman in a uniform. Although in this instance, that circumstance will not serve to help me choose between you and Mr. FitzClarence, for you must know, I have also seen you in uniform."

"Impossible." Ethan turned his head for a moment and searched her face to see if she was in jest. She appeared in earnest. "That cannot be, for I sold out seven years ago."

"And I *came out* seven years ago."

"Do not try to bamboozle me into thinking that we met during your come-out, my girl, for I vow I would have remembered."

"Ho! Your vows, like your memory, my lord, are written upon the wind. Seven years ago we shared a waltz, and a mere two minutes after our dance ended, you had forgotten me completely."

"Colly, is this true? But why did you not tell me that we had met before?"

"And puff up your conceit that *I* remembered you when *you* had forgot me. I thank you, no."

"*My* conceit!" Though he scowled at her, the humor in his eyes belied the seriousness of his countenance. "Fine talk from a female who spouts Latin at a fellow on every occasion."

Colly kept her face straight, but not without difficulty. Then, as he continued to regard her, she cautioned, "Have a care how you look at me, Lord Raymond, or I might suspect that you number among those of your sex who stare better than they think."

"No, no. Mind your semantics, Miss Bluestocking; the word I used was *ogle*. And if you mean to accuse me of ogling, my dear, I must insist that you no longer try to keep from laughing by pursing your lips in that utterly delightful manner. It quite drives all rational thought from my head. All thought," he added softly, "save one."

Colly's heart very nearly thumped its way out of her chest. She dared not even let herself guess at the meaning of his words. "Ethan, I—"

"There it be, m'lord," the tiger shouted, reminding Colly that she and Ethan were not alone. "There to the left. Just like the h'instructions said."

Only now did Colly take note of the stonework wall that was set back from the road. Wearing generations worth of gray lichens here and green mosses there, the wall ran for a goodly way before it divided to reveal large wrought iron gates and a private carriage drive. Since the gates stood open, making a stop unnecessary, Ethan guided the horses to the left, then tooled up the straight gravel drive toward the house.

The Kittridge home was not built on a grand scale, a gentleman's residence only, but it was of great an-

tiquity and very well cared for. Two stories in the
main edifice, with single-story wings to left and
right. The half-timbered building was a blend of
pleasing colors, with its blackened oak timber, its
gray slate roof, and its stonework mellowed to a
lovely pink.

The grass of the park was recently scythed, and
the shrubbery was well tended. Only the roses ran
wild, and they seemed to have been given their way
for many years, for they grew in profusion all around
the entrance to the house, their shoots rising up to
the sills of the mullioned windows only to spill
groundward once again.

The air was filled with the sweet aroma of the
roses, and Colly availed herself of it. "Umm," she
murmured, breathing her fill, "that is sheer heaven."

Ethan reined in the horses and waited as the tiger
jumped down and ran to their heads. He had only
just started to alight from the Tilbury when a white-
haired butler hastened out to ask if he could be of
service.

Ethan handed the servant his card. "This is Miss
Sommes," he said, "and we are here to see Mrs. Kittridge."

"Good afternoon, miss. My lord," the butler said,
bowing politely. "I fear the family is from home at
the moment. The little ones, you must know, have
been cooped up with the chicken pox, and it being
such a fine day, the mistress and the governess, Miss
Polteney, took them for an alfresco nuncheon over
near the Roman Bridge."

"Actually," Ethan explained, "we have no wish to

disturb the family. Miss Sommes is desirous of having a moment of conversation with her abigail, one Norah Cheswick."

"Yes," Colly interrupted. "If you would be so kind as to ask Norah to step out here for a moment, then I—"

"Begging your pardon, miss, but Norah ain't here. She's gone."

"Not here?" Colly repeated. "You mean she has gone with the family to help with the nuncheon?"

"No, miss. She has returned to London. Left this morning, she did. On the stage. With the children being on the mend, the mistress felt that Norah should return to Lady Sommes. First thing this morning, young Jem hitched up the trap and drove Norah to the inn. He put her on the stage himself. More 'n likely, you passed her on the road."

"Not here." Colly felt as if Fate mocked her with that phrase. Every time she thought the ring was within her reach, one of the gods capriciously transported it someplace else . . . someplace *not here*.

"Yes, ma'am," the butler replied. "More 'n likely, Norah is halfway back to London by now."

Chapter 11

The return to town was accomplished with very little conversation. Too disappointed at not getting the ring, Colly could think of nothing to say. Many times during the past twenty-four hours she had enacted a scene in her mind—a scene in which she handed the betrothal ring to Ethan with a flourish, accompanying the act with some appropriate remark. Each time, in her imagination, he had taken the ring, smiled at her, then told her that now they could be friends . . . now there were no barriers to their becoming more than friends.

She had so enjoyed that scene. But, of course, imagination had not become reality. And, sadly, it probably never would.

As they returned to the road that wound its way through Aymesley, cut through Wimbledon, then continued on to town, a new possibility crept into Colly's thoughts. A worrisome possibility. It was not a completely new idea, simply one that had lain dormant at the back of her mind—a contingency that had not seemed at all likely. Yet, suddenly, here it

was, rising from its dormancy, demanding to be reckoned with.

*What if Norah was no longer in possession of the
ring?*

Just thinking about that possibility made Colly
shiver with a cold fear. And rightly so, for people lost
jewelry every day. Colly knew that all too well. Several years ago she had lost a gold locket—an heirloom of both sentimental and monetary value. A
frenzied search had ensued, with Sommes Grange
being examined from kitchen to attics. No corner escaped close scrutiny. Still, the necklace had never
been found. Colly had always treated the locket with
special care, being fully aware of its value, yet she
had still lost it.

Norah, on the other hand, had no reason to believe the ring Gilly had given her was of any particular worth. If Gilly thought it a mere gewgaw, it was
only logical that the abigail would think the same.
Furthermore, it was a large gem, one that might easily become a nuisance; Norah might have removed
the ring to do some chore, then set it down someplace or other and forgotten all about it.

Or worse yet, the stage to London might have
been waylaid by footpads—such things still happened, even in these modern times. What if the
stage was stopped and the hapless passengers were
robbed of their money and jewels?

With such pictures in her mind, Colly grew quite
frightened. She wanted desperately to have the Bradford Diamond safe in her hands—no, she wanted it
safe in Ethan's hands. He was the owner, after all,

and the stone was worth a king's ransom. Colly balled her hands into fists to keep them from shaking, wondering what she would do if she never recovered the ring.

Actually, she knew very well what the result would be: Her father would feel obliged to pay restitution to the Bradford family. Ethan would not sue her, of course; having come to a fair evaluation of his character, Colly was convinced that he had made that threat only in the heat of anger. But his forgiveness of the loss would not satisfy Sir Wilfred. A true gentleman, her father would never let another bear the burden for something he believed was his debt.

Colly was forced to swallow a painful lump in her throat. Sir Wilfred was before-hand with the world, but his estate was not large enough to cover the cost of the Bradford Diamond. To do so would ruin him.

The only comfort to be had in the return trip was that Ethan, for some reason, had chosen not to mention the subject of the ring. Although that was something of a puzzle, as he had most certainly meant to question her about it yesterday. Whatever his reasons for delaying the catechism, however, Colly could only be grateful.

For Ethan's part, he felt Colly's distress and wished she would tell him what had overset her. There was more to this than simple disappointment at not being able to speak with the maid. Though from Colly's demeanor he knew that seeing the abigail had been a matter of some importance to her.

Surely, he thought, Colly must know that he would do anything in his power to help her. She had only to tell him what she required. But she said nothing. She sat quietly, her hands balled into tight little fists and her beautiful chin lifted proudly. She offered up no confidences. She asked for no help.

With no other options available, Ethan took his lead from his passenger and confined his conversation to one or two questions regarding her comfort. Her responses were polite but brief—so different from her usual vivacity—affording no openings for confidences. When she refused his offer to stop for a nuncheon at a small inn just outside Wimbledon, her voice distracted, he realized she was anxious to be back in town. Knowing that, he gave the horses their head, completing the journey as quickly as possible.

They arrived at Grillon's Hotel scarcely more than an hour later, at which time Ethan tossed the reins to the tiger, then helped Colly alight from the Tilbury. Hoping that a moment of privacy might make her feel free to confide in him, he escorted her through the almost deserted foyer and up the grand stairway. The sound of their footsteps was muffled by the carpeted stairs, the hush seeming to emphasize Colly's silence.

In the privacy of the hallway, just before they reached the door to her suite, Ethan caught her elbow, the gentle pressure bidding her to stop. He spoke softly. "I wish you would tell me what has made you so unhappy, little bluestocking."

She would not look at him. "Everything is fine, I assure you."

Obliged to accept her word, he caught her hand

and held it between both of his. Even through her glove he could feel the coolness of her skin, the trembling of her fingers. "I will not plague you to share more than you are comfortable doing, but if you should have need of a friend, Colly, please believe that I am yours to command."

When her gaze remained fixed somewhere in the vicinity of his cravat, Ethan placed his finger beneath her chin, then gently tipped her face upward, obliging her to look at him. The sadness in her lovely eyes did strange things to that life-sustaining organ beneath his cravat, making it pump frantically. Other parts of his anatomy were affected similarly as he noticed the slight trembling of her full, soft lips. His senses bewitched by her nearness and this strange new desire to protect her from life's vagaries, he was obliged to fight the urge to take her in his arms and mold her slender body against the length of his.

Controlling his desires, he offered sincerely, "If you can bring yourself to trust me, I promise you I will do all within my power to return that beautiful smile to your lips."

"Ethan. I—" Colly's voice broke, and needing no further inducement, he moved to slip his arm around her waist, to offer her the comfort of his shoulder.

Unfortunately, before he was able to turn her toward him, the door to the suite was snatched open. Instantly, Colly pushed free of his embrace, and he had, perforce, to let her go.

"Lord Raymond," Miss Gilly Sommes gasped, surprised to encounter someone just outside the door.

"Well met, Miss Gilly," he said, taking the young lady's hand and bringing it to his lips to divert her attention while Colly composed herself. "Allow me to compliment you upon your bonnet. A totally charming confection, to be sure. Celestial blue, like your eyes."

"Actually, it is lapis blue," she informed him, dimpling coquettishly. "My eyes are not nearly so dark." At the sound of footsteps behind her, Gilly called over her shoulder, "Mama, here is Colly, returned at last. And Lord Raymond is with her."

Lady Sommes and Miss Kittridge joined them at the door. Once the amenities were completed, Colly's mother said, "We are just on our way out, my dear, but if you wish to offer Lord Raymond some refreshment, we can certainly postpone our outing."

Ethan looked at Colly for guidance. When she lowered her eyelids, as if to deny him without having to give voice to the words, he directed his attention to Lady Sommes. "I would not wish to delay your excursion, ma'am. And I am persuaded that Miss Sommes is fatigued from our own outing. Delightful though we found it."

"Yes, delightful," Colly repeated, forcing a smile to her lips for the benefit of her relatives.

Unaware of her older sister's distress, the beautiful Gilly offered a suggestion of her own. "I have an idea, Lord Raymond. Since my sister is too fatigued to offer you refreshments, why do not you come with us? We are promised at the modiste's for fittings, but we are going for ices afterward." She looked up at Ethan, flirting in a quite outrageous manner, with

her eyes open wide and her mouth in a pretty half
smile. "I am persuaded you would find the modiste's
most interesting, my lord."

A giggle escaped Miss Kittridge.

"Gilly," her mother cautioned, disapproval in her
tone, "try for a little decorum. I am confident that
Lord Raymond will find nothing to like in such forward behavior."

Ethan bowed over Lady Sommes' hand. "I assure
you, ma'am, Miss Gilly is always a pleasure, as are
all the ladies of your family."

"Is Norah here?" Colly asked, surprising them all
with this seeming non sequitur.

"Why, no," her mother replied. "Did you not find
her at Mrs. Kittridge's?"

Colly shook her head. "Mrs. Kittridge had no further need of her, since the children were feeling
much better, so she sent her here on the morning
stage. I thought she would have arrived by now."

"Well, I must say," interrupted Gilly. "I find it unbelievably selfish in Norah not to have come
straight here, for I had need of her." She stretched
forward her left arm, inviting all to witness a slight
mend in the sleeve of her apple green pelisse. "Only
look at that; the hotel maid is possessed of cow
thumbs when plying a needle and thread."

No one but Miss Kittridge found the condition of
the sleeve of particular interest.

After giving her younger daughter a speaking
glance, Lady Sommes turned to explain to her other
daughter why they had no knowledge of the maid's
whereabouts. "We visited Grafton House earlier in the

day seeking gloves of a particular shade of primrose, and Norah may well have arrived while we were from the hotel. Though we heard nothing of her arrival. Since your aunt did not go with us, choosing rather to resume her vigil royal in the ladies' reading room, she may know more than I. Let us hope so, for we would all be distressed if anything has happened to Norah."

"Is Aunt Pet still in the reading room?"

"No," Lady Sommes replied, "she has lain down upon her bed, but she bade me tell you she is most anxious for a private word with you. She said it was important."

"Very well, I will go to her right away." She offered Ethan her hand, then thanked him once again for driving her to Aymesley.

"My pleasure," he assured her. "May I wait upon you tomorrow to assure myself that you are recovered from your fatigue?"

Colly's only answer was a silent nod.

"That would be famous," Gilly replied for her sister. "Meanwhile, we will walk down with you, for I am told you have a bang-up new Tilbury."

"Gilly!" Lady Sommes expostulated. "Let me hear no more cant from your lips."

With no way to refuse the chit's request, and quite certain that Colly wished him gone, Ethan escorted the ladies down the stairs; then, after allowing Gilly a moment to admire his carriage, he took himself back to Raymond House.

As soon as the foursome turned to walk down the hall, Colly shut the door to the suite, tossed her reticule and bonnet on a table in the sitting room, then hurried to the bedchamber shared by Lady Sommes and Miss Montrose. Just before she tapped at the door, she said a quick prayer that her aunt had indeed heard something from Norah.

"Aunt Pet?" she called softly. "are you asleep?"

"Come in, my dear. I have been waiting for you this hour and more."

While Colly opened the door and stepped inside the chamber, the older lady sat up, placed a pillow behind her back, then reached up to remove a riband from around her neck. "You will wonder, my dear, why I have taken to wearing ribands at my age, but once you see what is suspended from the gros-grain, you will appreciate my desire to keep the object secure."

Colly stepped closer to the bed, blinking in disbelief at the single piece of jewelry that rested rather incongruously in the hollow of her aunt's dear, though wrinkled, throat. "Oh, Aunt," she said breathlessly. "Please tell me I have not fallen asleep and am dreaming this. Is that . . . can it be . . . of course that must be . . . Oh, Aunt!"

Having finished her one-sided and somewhat disjointed conversation, Colly plopped down on the edge of the bed and hid her face in her hands. "Oh, Aunt," she said again, her voice betraying the tears that slipped between her fingers.

"Here, child," Miss Montrose said, pulling one of her niece's hands away from her face and placing the beribboned ring in the tear-dampened palm. "This wayward diamond has found its way back at last. Now we may rest easy."

Colly sniffed inelegantly. "You ca—cannot know how frightened I had become. I feared it had been lost forever. I am so—so relieved."

Miss Montrose laid her hand upon her niece's bowed head for a moment, murmuring such phrases as might comfort a young lady in the throes of such extreme relief.

When the bout of tears was nearly finished, the elder lady said, " 'Tis well for my nap that the ring is recovered, for I readily perceive that the bed linens would have been truly soaked had Norah come back empty-handed. Or more to the point, empty-fingered."

In spite of her tears, Colly laughed at her aunt's foolishness. In a short time her sobs had diminished to only an occasional watery hiccough, a circumstance that made the lachrymose lady happy to make use of her aunt's proffered handkerchief. "I still cannot believe the ring is here."

Even though her sight was distorted by the tears that lingered in her lashes, Colly stared at the ring in her hand. Contrary to the tales regarding its size, it was not as big as a doorknob. It was, however, the largest single diamond she had ever seen.

"Do you like it, Aunt Pet?" she asked, apropos of nothing.

"It wants cleaning. Aside from that, it is a most impressive gem. And I feel certain that any young lady so fortunate as to be the object of Lord Raymond's affection would not care one whit if the ring snagged her stockings or ruined her gloves."

Since this quite innocuous remark brought a fresh flood of tears, Miss Montrose took the ring from Colly's hand, matched up the ends of the ribbon, then tied the grosgrain around her niece's neck.

"Now, my dear, as you are finally in possession of that object for which we journeyed to town, I will leave you to do what you think best with it. And you will, if you please, leave me to my nap. All this racketing about town has left me in need of some quiet."

Colly gave her aunt a hug so fierce it called forth a complaint from the recipient. "Mind my bones, dear girl, for I had hoped to have the use of them for another two score years."

"Oh, no," Colly said, "I insist you make that three score, at the very least. For what would I do without my beloved Aunt Pet?"

"Pshaw," said her aunt, her cheeks a bright red at the demonstration of affection, "such flummery. Now leave me in peace, there's a good girl. And mind you find something appropriate in your jewelry box for Norah. She was most gracious in giving up her claim to the Bradford Diamond, and I cannot but think that she deserves something rather nice for her forbearance."

"You are wise, as always, Aunt Pet. I shall see to it right away. Where is Norah?"

"I sent her upstairs to the servant's rooms. She was fagged out from attending the three young Kittridges, and was in no frame to be tossed like a sacrificial lamb into Gilly's beastly clutter."

"You always know the right thing to do."

The compliment fell on deaf ears, for Miss Montrose had already settled herself once again beneath the covers and pulled a pillow over her head. Far from taking the action in bad part, however, Colly tossed a kiss in the direction of the shape beneath the covers, then tiptoed from the room.

Once she had reached the privacy of her bedchamber, she found her sister's portable writing desk, from which she removed a piece of vellum and a usable nib. After considering her words for only a minute or two, she composed a letter to Lord Raymond.

> Ethan,
>
> I am returning your betrothal ring. You have been most patient with me, and I thank you for your forbearance.
>
> The next time this ring is bestowed upon a young lady, I pray that she is more worthy to wear it than the last recipient.
>
> I shall probably not see you again soon, for my aunt and I will return to the Grange on the morrow.
>
> *Adieux,*

She signed the letter with only her initial. Then while the ink dried on the page, she returned the portable desk to the spot beneath the bed that Gilly thought proper for such items. When a search of the room revealed nothing appropriate to hold the ring, Colly contented herself with one of the glove boxes stacked upon the dressing table. Dumping the primrose gloves onto the bed, she used the tissue paper to wrap the ring securely; then she folded the letter, placed it and the tissue paper inside the box, and tied the box shut with the grosgrain riband.

Returning to the sitting room, she rang for a footman to deliver the box to Lord Raymond's house in Grosvenor Square. Colly wished she could return the ring in person, but that was, of course, totally out of the question. She might as well tie her garter in public as to present herself at the door of a bachelor gentleman's home. Such unacceptable behavior would result in a scandal, not only ruining Colly's reputation but also blighting Gilly's chances of having a successful come-out.

It was a simple task to ring for a footman to deliver the packet. It was not so simple to stem the tears that sprang to Colly's eyes at the realization that now, with the Bradford Diamond in his possession, Ethan had no further reason to continue calling upon her.

There was an emptiness inside Colly's chest—an emptiness so painful it felt as if someone had actually removed her heart. And the thought of never again seeing Ethan's ruggedly handsome face, of never again watching mesmerized as he raised that right eyebrow in silent question, of never again hearing his deep, wonderful laughter, made the emptiness seem larger and even more painful.

Promising herself that she positively would not cry again, Colly threw herself upon the bed and proceeded to soak the pillow with her tears.

Ethan arrived at Raymond House only a few minutes after leaving Grillon's Hotel, and was quite surprised to see his front door thrown open before he had a chance to toss the reins to the tiger.

"My lord," said the butler, his usually impassive face as near to excited as Ethan had ever seen it. "You are home at last."

"What is amiss, Yardley?"

"Nothing amiss, my lord." The butler proffered a silver salver upon which reposed a letter bearing the seal of the prime minister's office. "This letter came about an hour ago, my lord, and I thought perhaps you might wish the lad to keep the Tilbury waiting."

Recognizing the seal of office, Ethan quickly tore open the letter and read through the single sheet. "It is from Lord Liverpool," he said before tossing the missive back onto the salver. "The earl has granted me an hour of his time this afternoon to discuss the recent legislation relating to education. I shall need to change my clothes before calling upon him."

"Mr. Norbridge has everything in readiness, my lord."

Ethan nodded his approval. Taking the front steps two at a time, he said, "While I dress, have the lad take the Tilbury back to the stable, harness a fresh horse, then bring the carriage back around for me.

Tell him to waste no time. We do not want to keep the prime minister waiting."

"No, indeed, my lord." The butler allowed himself a brief smile, for like all the staff, he knew how important this meeting was to his master. "We shan't keep the prime minister waiting a moment longer than can be helped."

Ethan bounded up the stairs to the master bedchamber, where he found his valet waiting for him, a pitcher of hot water at the ready. "Well, Norbridge, we have word at last."

"I am pleased to say that we have, my lord," said the very proper gentleman's gentleman. "All is ready for you." Without need for words, the valet stripped the coat from his master's broad shoulders, tossing the article across the bed, then knelt to remove the top boots.

With a speed learned while in the army, Ethan undressed, refreshed himself, then redressed in the proper attire of gray coat, dark pantaloons, and white small clothes, all in less than ten minutes. He was arranging a fresh cravat when Yardley brought him a glass of Madeira and a plate of sandwiches. "To tide you over, my lord."

"Thank you, Yardley." After allowing himself time for only one large bite of sandwich, Ethan tossed back the Madeira, then turned to receive his gray gloves, his curly brimmed beaver, and his silver-handled cane from the valet.

"If you will excuse the presumption, my lord," the butler said, "Mr. Norbridge and I both wish you

the very best of good fortune in your meeting with
the prime minister."

"It is the children who need the good fortune, but
I thank you both for your wishes on my behalf."
Having said that, Ethan reached inside the pocket of
the coat he had only minutes ago discarded, retrieved a folded linen handkerchief, and placed it in
the inside pocket of his gray coat, next to his heart.

Startled, the valet looked about him in some confusion. "A thousand pardons, my lord. I must be all
about in my head; I thought I had supplied you with
a fresh handkerchief."

"You did," Ethan said, patting the pocket that now
held the handkerchief containing Colly's curl, "but
this one brings me luck."

Ethan had only just driven away when the footman from Grillon's arrived with the packet from
Colly. "This be for his lordship," the footman said,
showing the box to the butler, then quickly returning
it to the pocket of his coat to let Yardley know it was
not part of his design to relinquish it to any other
hand than Lord Raymond's.

Since the Sommes ladies had arrived at the hotel,
the footman had been on the receiving end of his
lordship's largesse on more than one occasion, and
he had every intention of collecting once again. "The
lady said as how I was to put this into no hand but
Lord Raymond's. And that's what I mean to do."

Yardley lifted his decidedly Roman nose in a way
that any member of his staff would have known im-

mediately meant he would brook no impertinence from lesser beings.

The footman was not impressed. "You can save them sour faces for brining pickles," he advised the butler. "I got my job same as you got yours, and mine is to give this here packet to his lordship."

"You impertinent looby," Yardley began, happily availing himself of several animadversions regarding the appearance and intelligence of London-bred servants. Unfortunately, he was denied the remainder of his set down by the arrival of Lady Raymond's carriage.

"What is this?" she demanded as the carriage pulled up at the curb.

Pushing the footman aside, the butler hurried down the stairs to hand her ladyship from her coach.

"Here now!" the footman said, regaining his balance and straightening his coat indignantly. "I'll thank you to keep your mitts to yourself. You ain't got no call to go scuttling my nob. I come here honest like to deliver summat to his lordship."

"And I told you, my good man, that his lordship is from home."

"You never did!"

Lady Raymond started up the stairs, paying little heed to the incensed footman. "My son has not returned yet, Yardley?"

"Yes, m'lady, he has returned. But then his lordship went out again."

The footman, perceiving that the tip he had hoped for was dissolving into thin air, decided to try another tack. "Your ladyship," he began. "Begging your pardon, ma'am, but I got an important packet for his lordship, and this here Friday-faced butler is—"

"Here now," the butler interjected, "be off with you before I have you thrown off the premises."

"But Miss Sommes said as how—"

"Did you say Sommes?" Lady Raymond asked. She had just set one foot inside the elegant foyer with its black and white marble floor, but she stopped and turned to look at the footman.

Not slow to notice the interest in the older lady's eyes, the man replied, "Yes, m'lady. Miss Sommes give me this packet to deliver into his lordship's own hand." He removed the box from his pocket but, as before, held it just out of reach. "Had tears in her eyes, the young lady did." He said no more, only waited to see if this latest piece of information would pique her ladyship's interest.

It did.

"I am Lady Raymond. I am persuaded Miss Sommes will have no objections to my receiving the packet." She extended her gloved hand, then said to the butler, "Give the man something for his trouble, Yardley."

"Yes, m'lady."

Satisfied, the footman held the packet out. It was quickly snatched from his hand by the irate butler, who presented it to his mistress. Whereupon, Lady Raymond disappeared inside the house, leaving the servants to settle the matter in their own way.

If the footman had only known just how much Lady Raymond's interest was piqued by the mention of Miss Sommes' tears, he might have held out for the big gratuity he had originally envisioned. Unfortunately, he would never know with what speed her ladyship adjourned to the book room to study the packet, placing it on her son's massive desk, then seating herself in the chair just behind the desk.

I knew there was something between Miss Sommes and my son! she thought triumphantly. *Never mind that silly gibberish Ethan tried to make me believe. A mother knows her own children.*

Her eyes alight with curiosity, Lady Raymond lifted the nearly weightless box and shook it. It made no sound. *But what can this mean?* The delivery of a glove box bearing the logo of Grafton House and tied up with a hair riband was enough to make any mother curious. It was not to be wondered at, then, that such a delivery, coupled with the further knowledge that the sender had been in tears, quite sent the curious mother over the edge.

Convincing herself that it was her maternal duty to protect her son's interests, Lady Raymond so forgot herself as to retrieve scissors from the desk drawer and snip the riband in two. First she opened the single sheet of vellum and read through the brief message. Her only reaction to the words was a gasp. Then, her hands trembling, she dropped the letter and tore open the tissue paper. The Bradford Diamond fell onto the desk blotter with a soft thud.

"No," Lady Raymond whispered, her eyes suddenly abrim with tears, "that foolish, foolish gel. I will not allow her to jilt Ethan in this manner, for it will break his heart."

Leaving the letter on the desk beside the box and

torn tissue paper, she slipped the ring onto her pinky finger, remembering just in time how snug it had been for her when she had worn it years ago. Then, too impatient to ring the bell, she ran to the doorway and yelled for the butler. "Yardley!"

"Yes, m'lady?"

"Send someone around to have my carriage brought back immediately. I must go to Grillon's Hotel. I must do what I can to save my son."

Chapter 12

Colly was not normally such a watering pot, and after allowing herself a good cry, she took her emotions in hand and rose from the bed. She had only just finished washing her face and was in the process of changing her sadly wrinkled traveling dress when there came a soft scratch at the bed-chamber door.

"Miss Colly," Norah said softly. "Are you awake?"

"Come in, Norah."

"There be a lady to see you, Miss Colly. I asked did she wish to see Lady Sommes or Miss Montrose, on account of her not being a young lady, but she said she had come to see you. And see you she would, she said, or know the reason why."

"How very odd. Did the lady not give her name?"

The abigail shook her head. "If she did, I never heard it." She lowered her voice lest she be over-heard. "And if you'll forgive my saying so as shouldn't, miss, the lady be in quite a taking."

Colly turned her back so the abigail could help

her with the tapes of her lavender dress. "Surely you do not mean she is angry?"

"In a pure pet. Mad as hops, as my Fa was used to say. I bid her be seated, but she refused, choosing instead to pace back and forth across the sitting room. Fair wearing a path in the turkey carpet, she be."

Colly knew a sudden craven impulse to instruct the abigail to deny her to whoever was abusing the hotel's carpet. She wanted no further emotional scenes, having had quite enough for one day. However, since it was not in her nature to ask the servants to fight her battles for her, she took a quick glance at herself in the looking glass to make certain her hair was reasonably neat, then squared her shoulders and went out to the sitting room.

Her courage almost deserted her when she espied Lady Raymond. Norah had assessed the situation correctly. Ethan's mother was most definitely in a pet.

"Lady Raymond," Colly began, "good afternoon. It is a pleasure to—"

"Do not try to turn me up sweet with that innocent look, my gel, for I know what you have done."

Startled, Colly took a step back. "Ma'am? I am sure I do not know—"

"How could you behave in such a cruel manner? I had thought better of you."

Before Colly could ask for elucidation, her ladyship's plump face crumpled and she burst into tears.

"Lady Raymond," Colly said, hurrying to the visitor's side to take her arm and lead her to the sofa. "Please, ma'am, rest a moment while I have the maid fetch us some refreshment. I am persuaded you will feel more the thing once you have a cup of tea."

With a wave of her now sodden lace handkerchief, Lady Raymond refused the offer. "A cup of tea will not revive my spirits," she said between sniffs, "nothing can. Nothing, that is, save your promise to reconsider your thoughtless actions. For I assure you, young woman, you have dealt me a wounding blow."

Wondering if she was, perhaps, still asleep on her bed, Colly balled her hands into fists and pressed her fingernails into the soft flesh of her palms. No, she was awake! "Ma'am, I have no notion what I could have done to overset you so. Though it distresses me that any action of mine—thoughtless or not—could bring you to tears. Whatever I have done, I do most humbly beg your pardon."

Colly sat down beside the visitor and took one of the lady's hands in hers. "If you could bring yourself to tell me what I have done, perhaps I could rectify it. Or, at least, explain my actions."

Not nearly as tall as Colly, Lady Raymond was obliged to look up. Tears shimmered on her lashes. "Can you explain why you have broken my son's heart?"

Colly felt a shudder run through her. This was madness. If anyone's heart was broken, it was hers. Ethan had what he wanted, the ring. It was she who had nothing—nothing save a few brief memories and a future of loneliness. A future without Ethan. Her throat ached with the effort to hold back her tears.

Receiving no reply to her question, Lady Raymond

snatched her hand from Colly's. "How could you be so cruel as to jilt Ethan?"

Jilt? "Lady Raymond, I am afraid you have been misinformed. I have not jilted Ethan. I could not, for the simple reason that we are not betrothed."

The older lady's cheeks grew quite pink with anger. "Do not try to flummox me. Ethan tried that trick and it would not serve. A mother knows these things. One has only to observe him as he looks upon you to see the depth of the sentiments my son cherishes."

Colly felt her own face grow warm. "I assure you, ma'am, you mistake the matter."

"Do you take me for a fool? It is written plain on both your faces. He loves you. You love him. There cannot be two opinions on the subject."

For just a moment Colly's heart seemed to stand still. Surely his mother was mistaken. Ethan did not love her. *True*, she loved him, but . . . No. It was something his mother had misread.

"And if you are trying to think up some other Banbury tale," Lady Raymond continued, "I take leave to inform you, missy, that I am not to be trifled with."

Having said this, her ladyship held up her hand, palm toward her heart, and began rapidly moving her fingers. "You see, my gel, I have the proof right here."

Her mind in a state of turmoil, it took Colly a moment to realize the wiggling fingers were meant to signify something. Suddenly she espied the Bradford

Diamond. She recoiled, almost as if the lady wore something sinister upon her pinky.

"Ah ha! Caught at last, Miss Sommes. Deny this if you can."

"How did you . . .?"

"Ethan is from home," she replied, "I accepted the packet you sent."

Colly could not believe her ears. "Never tell me that you opened it."

"And read your letter," she said, her tone a fine mixture of anger and self-justification.

"But . . . the letter was meant only for Ethan's eyes. I cannot believe you read it."

Lady Raymond puffed up like a partridge. "You may save your reproaches, for believe me, I will do anything to protect my sons. It was a fortunate thing that I intercepted that packet while Ethan was from home. Now I have time to bring you to a realization of the error you have made. You cannot break this engagement; you must take back the ring."

Colly struggled to maintain her composure. If she was not so exasperated, she would have laughed. What a coil. Once again she was being mistaken for the recipient of the betrothal ring; and once again she could not defend herself without betraying her sister. The only difference in the circumstances was that this time, the person confronting her was angry because she had *returned* the ring.

"Ma'am," she said as gently as she could. "Do not you think this is a matter best left between Ethan and me?"

At the gentle tone, all the anger seemed to slip

away from Lady Raymond. "But you left me no choice when you took the coward's way out and broke the betrothal by mail. How could you do so? I had thought you such a kind gel. And so totally suited to my son."

Colly was in such complete agreement with this last statement that she nodded her head without realizing what she was doing.

"I knew it!" Lady Raymond said. "You do love him. No point in denying it, young lady, for it is plain as a pikestaff."

Colly had no intention of denying it; in fact, she decided that her wisest option was to keep her tongue between her teeth and say nothing more. Anything she said at this point might trip her up. She risked betraying Gilly, and even worse, she risked revealing the love she felt for Ethan Bradford. A love he did not return—no matter what his doting mother thought.

Lady Raymond slipped the ring from her pinky and held it between her thumb and forefinger, turning it in a manner that made it catch the light. Blue fire seemed to flash from each facet. "It is beautiful, is it not?"

"Yes, ma'am," Colly answered softly, "it is."

"I wore this ring when I was betrothed. Did Ethan tell you," she asked, "that my marriage to his father was a love match?"

Colly shook her head, not wanting to reveal that Ethan had told her nothing of his family.

"I loved my husband with my whole being," she continued. "And I have always insisted that my sons settle for nothing less than that same kind of alliance. Marriage without love is insupportable. Do not you agree?"

In complete agreement with that sentiment, Colly said, "Yes, ma'am."

With tears in her eyes, Lady Raymond reached for Colly's hand. Thinking Ethan's mother sought comfort, Colly let her hand be taken, but before she had time to comprehend what was happening, Lady Raymond had forced the betrothal ring onto the third finger of Colly's left hand.

"Madam!"

Instinctively, Colly reached to pull the ring from her finger. Unfortunately, she could not get it to slip back over her knuckle. She twisted it, turned it, pulled it. It would not budge. "It is stuck fast!"

"Good," Lady Raymond replied. "Now you will be obliged to wear it a while longer. I trust you will use the time wisely; reconsider whatever foolishness you have gotten into your head. And foolishness it is. For I assure you, my dear, Ethan would not want you to end this engagement."

She reached over and patted Colly's face. "You will make him an excellent baroness."

Now all smiles, Lady Raymond gathered her reticule and her sodden handkerchief and walked to the door. "I must be going," she said happily, "for I am promised to Lady Wessingham this evening for dinner and a card party." She opened the door but stopped just on the threshold to blow a kiss to Colly. "Good-bye, my dear, dear girl."

Pleased with the outcome of his meeting with the prime minister, Ethan returned to Raymond House with only one thought in his mind: to go see Colly to share with her what had transpired. Of course, she was expecting him to call upon her on the morrow, but that was several hours away, and he did not think he could wait until then. He wanted to see her now.

Of late, he had found himself wanting to share with Colly every thought in his head, every feeling in his heart, every event of his life down to the smallest detail. He smiled, remembering her quickness, her ability to see right to the heart of a matter. He could always count upon her to see the humor of a situation, or the seriousness. And, he thought, the smile turning to one of resignation blended with admiration, he could also count on her to praise him only when praise was due and to depress pretension should he credit himself with more acumen than he ought.

Yes, I must see my lovely bluestocking.

Thinking it wise to send around a note first, he went into his book room to compose a request that Colly allow him to escort her to dinner in the hotel dining room. He had only just sat down at the desk when he espied a slender box and a quantity of torn tissue paper strewn about the blotter. About to brush the clutter aside, he noticed the single sheet of vellum and picked it up, reading through it only once before searching through the paper for the ring. Finding nothing, he went to the bell pull to summon the butler.

"Yardley," he said when the servant knocked, then opened the door, "a packet arrived for me this afternoon. What do you know of it?"

"It was delivered just after you left for your appointment with Lord Liverpool, sir."

"And you put it on my desk?"

"No, my lord, her ladyship received the packet."

Not by as much as a raised eyebrow did the butler show that he was aware of the mess on the desk. "Shall I send a maid to her ladyship's chamber to inquire after it?"

Ethan shook his head. "Thank you, I will take care of the matter."

Leaving the servant to think what he would, Ethan bound up the elegantly curving staircase and knocked at his mother's door. Lady Raymond's dresser answered his knock, and at his abrupt nod for her to leave the room, the woman slipped silently into the dressing room adjoining the chamber and closed the door.

"Ethan, you have returned. I—" Seeing her son's unsmiling face, Lady Raymond put her hand to her throat, the ruffles of her lace wrapper fluttering as she lifted her arm. "Dear boy, what is the matter?"

"You tell me," he said quietly, stepping over to a satin-covered *bergère* chair and resting his hands upon the curved top. "Did you find everything you needed in my book room?"

"Your book room? Why should I—" His mother

had the grace to blush. "I daresay you are referring to the packet I opened. I had forgotten all about it, being much too happy when I returned to worry with such things."

"Oh, but you must worry about such things, Mother, for fundamentals are most important, especially if you are contemplating taking up the spy business—which, I conjecture, you must be doing." Lady Raymond tried to interrupt, but Ethan continued. "Always, and I cannot stress this too strongly, always leave things exactly as you find them. A good spy never expects the servants to clean up the mess. And you may wish to learn how to—"

"Ethan! Stop this. I know you are angry, and indeed you have every right to be—"

"True on both counts, ma'am."

"Well, I beg your pardon, I am sure. But I believed I was acting for the best. And, as it transpires, I was correct. A mother has instincts about such things."

"Ah, yes. Maternal instincts. If I may ask, what reckless act have those instincts led you to do this time?"

"Nothing you will dislike, I assure you. I merely visited Grillon's to have a talk with Miss Sommes."

Only the flexing of his hand upon the curve of the chair betrayed Ethan's anger. "And did you? Talk with her, I mean?"

A happy smile transformed his mother's face. "Yes, my dear, and I have made everything right again. She has agreed to honor her betrothal. I took the ring with me, and you will be pleased to know that your fiancée is wearing it as we speak."

Ethan's anger was being overridden by a strong inclination to laugh. "Miss Sommes is wearing my ring? May I hope, Mother, that you refer to Miss *Colly* Sommes and not to her younger sister. Their identities have been confused once before."

Lady Raymond made a sound suspiciously reminiscent of a snort. "Do not be absurd. *You*, interested in a silly young chit with nothing to recommend her but a pretty face? I know my sons better than that. 'Tis the kind of gel your brother would choose. Besides, one has only to witness you and Miss Colly Sommes together, forever gazing at each other and smelling of April and May. 'Tis plain as a pikesta—"

"Cut line, Mother. What did you do?"

"I told her that she would make you an excellent baroness, and then I put the betrothal ring on her finger."

Ethan could control his laughter no longer. "How very droll, to be sure. Since you have proposed for me and placed the ring upon the lady's finger, may I be so presumptuous as to inquire if Miss Sommes accepted my suit?"

His mother did not look directly at him. "As to that, I am afraid you and your betrothed have a few matters that need to be discussed between you. I cannot, after all, be expected to do everything."

"Naturally not, dear lady, how very unappreciative of me. But you say she *is* wearing the betrothal ring.

She did not, perhaps, snatch it off and throw it back in your face?"

"Of course not! Miss Sommes is a lady; she would never do anything so vulgar. Besides," his mother added with an impish grin, "the ring fits quite snugly. She could not get it off her finger."

Not very much later, while Ethan made his way to Grillon's Hotel, Colly and her aunt waited for a tea tray to be brought to them in their sitting room. Miss Montrose had only just noticed the ring upon her niece's finger and bade Colly explain why she was wearing the Bradford Diamond. "When I made certain, my dear, that you meant to return it with all haste to Lord Raymond."

"I did return it, Aunt Pet."

In a very few words Colly related the scene between herself and Lady Raymond. "And now I discover that as difficult as it was to get the ring into my hands, it is even more difficult to be rid of it."

"What mean you, child?"

Colly lifted her hand, spread her fingers, and attempted to remove the ring, demonstrating its snugness. "Try what I may, it will not slip over my knuckle. I have soaked my finger, I have rubbed the skin with cucumber lotion, and, at Norah's suggestion, I even coated my knuckle in butter. All to no avail."

"Well, of course not, my dear. You have worried the joint until it is swollen. Let it be; do not try to force the ring again. By tomorrow, you may believe me, the knuckle will be its usual size and you may remove the ring at that time."

"I trust you may be right, Aunt, for I had hoped to see what I could do to persuade you to return to Sommes Grange on the morrow. That is, if you have had enough of watching the royal courtships."

"To be sure, my dear, I have seen little aside from what is reported in the papers, and I could as easily read that at home. If the truth be told, I will not be loath to leave off sharing accommodations with your mother; so, if it will suit you to leave on the morrow, I am willing."

"But only," Colly cautioned, "If I am able to remove this ring. I wish to place it in Ethan's hand so that I may put the entire episode from my thoughts."

"And can you do that?" Miss Montrose asked quietly. "Forget the entire episode, I mean. I had thought Lord Raymond was becoming most particular in his attentions to you, my dear, and I will confess that I had cherished the hope that he would—"

"Would what?" Colly asked softly. "Ride up on his white charger? Scoop me into his arms? Then carry me off to his castle where we would live happily ever after? You are ever the romantic, Aunt."

"No, no. Acquit me, at least, of that hackneyed fantasy. I envisioned something more real for you, my dear. I wanted a gentleman who would appreciate you for the wonderful, intelligent gel you are. A gentleman who would share your life and make you an integral part of his life. A gentleman who would love you and, God willing, give you children. A gentleman such as Lord Raym—"

"Please, Aunt Pet. Do not."

Quietly, Miss Montrose added, "I had thought, my dear, that you were wishful of those same things."

"Perhaps I was. Once." Colly gazed at the diamond upon her finger; then, sighing, she slipped her hand beneath the folds of her skirt to remove the gem from her vision. "I pray you, Aunt, let us speak of this no more, for it is fatally easy to fall into such dreaming. And in this particular instance, the dream can never come true."

That point, Miss Montrose thought, was arguable. However, perceiving that her niece was close to tears, the older lady chose to keep her opinions safely hidden. Since Norah had just opened the door to bring in the tea tray, keeping her own council was even easier than it might have been. "Ah, Norah. Just in time."

Signaling for the abigail to bring the tray to her, Miss Montrose said, "Shall I pour, my dear?"

Roused from a brown study, Colly blinked her eyelids, then nodded. "But what is that folded beneath the plate of cakes, Aunt?"

Miss Montrose retrieved the single sheet of printed matter and opened it to its full size. "It is a broadside," she declared, her affronted tone giving evidence of her opinion. "And so very uncivil." She studied the drawing, then passed the broadside to her niece. "Only look at the caricature. It makes jest of the dukes of Clarence and Kent upon their coming nuptials."

Colly was hard pressed not to laugh at the satirical renditions of the two royal dukes and their future duchesses. The German princesses, their shy young faces covered by bridal veils, walked sedately down the aisle, while the dukes, with rather fatuous looks on their aged faces and a cradle under each arm, raced one another to the altar. The broadside was entitled, THE ROYAL RACE, WHO WILL PRODUCE THE HEIR?

"So exceedingly vulgar," Miss Montrose noted, "jesting about the royal marriages in that way."

"The writer is scarcely less charitable to the throng of society couples who are to be wed as soon as the royals are joined in matrimony." With a smile she read aloud: " 'Those couples who, like a gaggle of common geese, follow in the footsteps of the royal peacocks.' "

Perceiving no humor in the depiction, Miss Montrose remarked, "I never thought to say such a thing, but I am happy that neither of my nieces is betrothed at the moment. How lowering to be numbered among those common geese."

"Just so," Colly mumbled, thankful that her aunt had no talent for reading minds. For a moment there, Colly had been guilty of harboring an almost overpowering desire to join the gaggle.

Some twenty minutes later, Ethan knocked at the door to the Sommes' suite. Though he had quit Raymond House in quite good spirits, still laughing at his mother's machinations and the resulting "betrothal," he knew better than to expect Colly to see the situation in the same amused vein. He could well imagine the justifiably scathing remarks his beautiful bluestocking would heap upon his head the moment he arrived. He looked forward to bandying words with her.

To his surprise, however, his reception was not what he had expected. When the abigail admitted him to the sitting room, Colly looked at him for a fleeting instant, then lowered her gaze to her lap. Her lovely complexion was pink with embarrassment, and her left hand was shoved ignominiously beneath her lavender skirt.

The ring must still be wedged fast upon her finger, Ethan decided.

"Good evening, Miss Montrose. Miss Sommes."

"Lord Raymond," the older lady greeted soberly. "An unusual time for visiting, is it not?"

"Most unusual, ma'am. But unusual actions must occasion unusual reactions."

He turned his attention to Colly. She had not spoken, and if anything, her face had grown even pinker.

All humor now gone from his thoughts, Ethan decided he would do well to tread lightly. He wished to save the situation, not make it worse. "I had meant to send around a note begging you to have dinner with me downstairs, so that I might tell you of my visit with the prime minister. However, when I discovered that you had received a visit from my mother this afternoon, I decided not to wait upon ceremony."

At his reference to the prime minister Colly had lifted her gaze. But only for a moment. Ethan wished she would rail at him. Yell. Scream. Throw a vase at his head. Anything but this silence. "I can see that you are upset, my friend, and I hope you will believe that I am in sympathy with your feelings. For both our sakes, I am persuaded we should discuss my mother's visit. May we do so?"

Still not looking at him, Colly nodded her head, agreeing to his request.

Ever perceptive, Miss Montrose spoke to the abigail, informing that worthy that she wished a word in private with her in the bedchamber. "For you must know, Norah, that Miss Colly and I are decided upon quitting town first thing tomorrow. Pursuant to that, I wish to show you which of my dresses to pack."

If the abigail thought this an odd request from someone quitting a hotel, she made no comment, simply following Miss Montrose to the bedchamber.

"Colly," Miss Montrose said from the doorway, "if you have no objection, I will leave this door only slightly ajar, since I wish to speak with Norah in private. However, should you wish to gain my attention, you need only raise your voice a little, and I will hear you."

Grateful to the older lady for her generous spirit in allowing him to speak privately with her niece, Ethan wasted no time in drawing one of the side chairs close to the sofa where Colly sat. "I am sorry," he said softly. "Once again I must apologize for a member of my family. They seem to grow more reckless by the day."

Smiling, he reached forward and eased her left hand from beneath the folds of her skirt, revealing the large diamond. "Was the meeting so bad, my friend?"

Taking umbrage at his smile when she could find no humor in the situation, Colly tried to pull her hand away. Ethan would not let her go, and this annoyed her even more. To avoid a scene, she ceased to struggle, but giving in only increased her irritation. Finally, anger got the better of embarrassment and she found her voice.

"*Bad*, you ask? Why, not at all, sir. Except, of course, that I had no notion how I should behave. You will think this foolish in me, I am persuaded, but I have not previously been acquainted with a family whose peculiar standards of behavior included forever accusing me of being engaged to one or other of its members."

This is more like it, Ethan thought. This was the kind of biting reaction he had expected. Though he was careful to keep his elation to himself. "My poor girl," he muttered solicitously.

She ignored this remark. "Ah, but the reproaches do not end there. While you, sir, saw nothing amiss in accusing me of enticing a young boy, then further insulted me by threatening me with a lawsuit to guarantee the return of the betrothal ring, your mother was so kind as to accuse me of being a jilt. A cowardly one, no less—one who would jilt by the mail. Then she literally forced that same betrothal ring upon my finger."

"Totally reprehensible behavior," Ethan agreed cordially. "You have been sorely tried by my entire family. My poor, poor girl."

Unable to suffer this form of address a moment longer, Colly advised him to desist immediately. "For I will have you know that I am neither poor nor a girl."

"Yes, I know. Five-and-twenty, you said. And I believe you also informed me that you were not hanging out for a husband."

Almost betrayed into a giggle, Colly struggled to retain some semblance of composure. "How unhandsome of you to be constantly throwing my own words back into my teeth. Especially when I am in no frame of mind to retaliate as you deserve."

"Very bad form of me, to be sure. May I ask, my glorious creature, what you are in the frame of mind to do? Dare I hope I might like it? Could it be the same thing I have been in the frame of mind to do almost from the first moment I saw you?"

The beginnings of laughter shone in his eyes—laughter and something else, something Colly could not, would not put a name to. She dared not. She had, after all, been down this path once before. She would not deceive herself again into thinking Ethan's jesting foolishness was something of a warmer nature.

"Never mind my mind, sir. And release my hand, do."

Far from obeying her, he turned her hand over and

raised it to his lips, pressing slow, warm kisses inside her palm. "I see you are still wearing my ring," he said softly against her tingling skin.

"I cannot get it off," she muttered. The voice did not sound like her own, so occupied was she in resisting the desire to raise her other hand to his face to feel the rugged contours of his jaw.

"Good," he whispered. His mesmerizing lips having arrived at the inside of her wrist, he let the tip of his tongue trace her wildly beating pulse.

Colly forced her mind to ignore the sensations he was creating not only in her wrist, but also in the secret places of her body . . . and her soul. She needed to keep her wits about her. He had said, "Good." What did he mean? She was still trying to puzzle it out when he tossed her a seeming non sequitur.

"Does your family keep a list of flower names to be used in naming their daughters?"

Surely she had not heard him correctly. "A list?"

"Yes. Does one exist?"

Had he gone daft, or had she?

Somehow, without her even being aware of it, Ethan had moved from the chair to the sofa. Seating himself quite close to her, he slid his arm around her shoulders and gently drew her into the circle of his arm. As though the answer were important to him, he asked, "Is there some kind of order? If so, pray, what is the next name to be used?"

It was almost impossible to concentrate on this nonsense about lists when her head felt so right resting in the hollow of his broad shoulder. It was a simple matter to turn her face so that her cheek lay against his chest. She could hear his heart beating; it raced almost as fast as her own pulse. And she could smell that wonderful masculine fragrance that seemed to be coming from his skin.

To test the theory, she raised her hand and pushed his neck cloth aside a mere inch so she could press her face against the skin of his bare neck. His skin was so warm, the muscular column beneath so taut, so powerful it sent shivers coursing through her. Colly heard Ethan's indrawn breath, and somehow encouraged by the sound, she moistened her lips, then touched them to his warm skin.

He seemed to know exactly what she wanted, and obligingly drew her even closer to him, using both his strong arms to hold her fast. His lips touched her temple, his warm breath making a wayward curl dance across her forehead. "The name?" he reminded her.

"Why do you ask?"

"I have been picturing a little girl with your lovely skin." He slid his palm very slowly up Colly's arm, testing the skin for himself and practically searing her with his heat. "Lily might be a suitable name for such a child. Or," he added, warming to the theme, "if she inherited your beautiful gray-green eyes, Pansy might serve."

Colly resisted these heart-pleasing compliments with difficulty. Not wanting to delude herself that Ethan was suggesting what he seemed to be suggesting, she answered pertly, "The next name in line is Gloxinia."

After a moment of stunned silence Ethan threw

back his head and roared with laughter. "Gloxinia? Egad. Do you suppose, Miss Brassface, that you could bring yourself to break with tradition? Take pity on the poor child. Please, name her Rose."

Colly shook her head. "I fear not," she said, struggling hard to keep from joining in Ethan's laughter. "It is Gloxinia or nothing."

Ethan sighed loudly. "I know better than to attempt to dissuade you, madam, for I have firsthand experience of your family loyalty. If it must be Gloxinia, then so be it." Staring off into space, he said the name a few times aloud, as if experimenting with the feel and sound of it. "Gloxinia. Gloxinia. Hmm. Miss Gloxinia Bradford. It has a certain ring to it, you will agree."

Colly's lungs seemed to have atrophied; she could barely breathe. Ethan was proposing. This time she was not deluding herself. But did he love her? She had to know. For no matter how much she loved him, she would not sentence herself to a lifetime of heartache.

"Are you telling me that you need to start filling your nursery?" she asked rather timidly. "I know your mother feels it is time you married, but—"

"Colly," he said, shaking his head in disbelief, "that is the first time I ever heard you talk like an idiot."

Cupping her chin in his hand, he turned her face up so that she was obliged to look at him. "I want you to listen to me, Miss Columbine Sommes— daughter of Violet and future mother of, uh, Gloxinia—I wish to have no misunderstanding about this.

I, Ethan Delacourt Bradford, sixth Baron Raymond, am a man in love."

Colly lifted her hand and touched his angular jaw, as she had wanted to do earlier. "You are in love? With me?"

He nodded, catching sight of the diamond she wore on the hand cradling his face. "It is a gaudy bauble, I must admit, but I wish you would keep it, Colly. For after knowing you, I could never bestow it upon another woman."

He turned his face into her palm and kissed it once again. "Any other woman," he whispered against her skin, "would be only second best."

Here was a sentiment Colly could appreciate. Using both her hands, she turned Ethan's face so she could look into his eyes. What she saw there caused her to bestow upon him a smile warm enough to encourage any gentleman. "From the moment I met you, Ethan Bradford, all other men became second best."

Having heard all he needed, Ethan pulled her none too gently into his arms, crushing her against him as he had wanted to do almost from the first moment he saw her at Sommes Grange, with her glorious hair hanging down about her shoulders. "I have a confession," he said when he could spare his lips from the far more satisfactory job they had been doing against her neck, her eyelids, and finally her beautiful lips. "I have something that belongs to you."

As Colly watched, fascinated, he reached inside his coat, removed a linen handkerchief, then unfolded it carefully to reveal a lock of hair. Colly stared at the light brown curl, mystified.

"Ethan, how came you to have that? Surely it cannot be mine."

"Actually," he said, "it is mine. I have been keeping it until such time as I could persuade you to loosen your glorious mane and let me lose myself in it." He looked deeply into her gray-green eyes. "Will you do that for me, Colly? I ache to hold you in my arms and make you mine. Will you marry me, my love? Soon. Very soon."

"Marry?" With her heart racing madly, her mind seemed to have deserted her. Logical thought seemed an impossibility. She tried to think what to do. "I have nothing to wear," she said finally. "I shall have to borrow a dress from my mother."

Smiling, Ethan said, "You may borrow your father's trousers for all I care. I daresay you will probably try to wear them in our marriage."

"Never!"

"Liar," he said, following this compliment with a soft, lingering kiss.

When Ethan finally ended the kiss, he returned to the subject of the wedding clothes. "Though I am impatient to make you mine, my sweet, I think I can wait long enough for you to procure a dress of your own. Especially since I do not wish to share our wedding date with the royal dukes."

"Oh, no," Colly said, suddenly remembering the broadside and the writer's scathing commentary on the *common geese* who would be following the royals to the altar. "I may be a goose," she said, laughing, "but I do not wish to be a common one. Let us, by all means, give the royals their day."

By mutual consent they forsook the discussion of weddings for the far more interesting one of each other and their love. "Ethan," Colly said, twining her arms around his neck and looking up at him in a way that sorely taxed his resolve to delay the wedding by so much as an hour, "show me all the different ways there are to kiss."

Ethan's voice was a husky growl. "All the ways, my beautiful flower?"

"Oh, yes. I have loved you for so long, and now that I can hold you and kiss you, I regret all the days we have missed. *Hiatus valde deflendus*, you might say."

"I doubt I would say anything of the sort, my darling bluestocking. But if it is kisses you wish, kisses you shall have." Without further delay Ethan crushed her soft, willing body against his and applied himself to the delightful task of making up for lost time.